The Duel at Murphy's Ford

Eli Riley was the marshal of Murphy's Ford. It was a prosperous town, growing with the aid of copper mining and a peaceful place in which to live. Then something went wrong. The town's water supply was poisoned and folk became ill. Blame was laid on the copper company and trouble started when two prominent citizens were killed.

Then a stranger came to town, looking to avenge their deaths. Murphy's Ford was divided and a vigilante mob set out to make trouble for the mine owners. Marshal Riley found himself in a shoot-out that left him injured as the water poisoners became known and the demand for their lynching grew.

How would it all end?

The Duel at Murphy's Ford

Tom Benson

A Black Horse Western

ROBERT HALE · LONDON

Typeset by
Derek Doyle & Associates, Shaw Heath
Printed and bound in Great Britain by
Antony Rowe Limited, Wiltshire

ONE

Murphy's Ford was a prosperous place. The streets were busy and the railroad now came within twelve miles of the fast-growing township. It had all started in the days when gold mining was bringing folk to explore the creeks that fed the river. They had needed to get across the deep and fast-flowing water. That was where Shaun Murphy had hit upon an idea that gave him a steady income for the rest of his life.

He started off by rowing them across; his powerful arms did the work while the cheerful banter made them happy enough to pay his charges. Then he had the idea of placing a cable across the river and using a large floating platform that he could manage with a heave on the pullies attached to it. He could transport carts and horses, and a small town gradually grew up around the little hut that was his home.

The war came and went without much damage

being done to the growing community. Copperminers settled up in the hills as the demand filtered through from industry. The telegraph arrived. A bank was built, and the ranchers bought their necessities from the increasing number of stores. A mayor was chosen, and a jailhouse erected. Shaun Murphy lived long enough to find the little place named after him, and died a proud and not very sober man before things changed.

And they did change. The days of gold mining came to an end. Only a dozen or so prospectors still explored the creeks and made a bare living as they toiled in the hope of hitting some new bonanza. But the copper mining grew. Several hundred men, many of them Chinese, were employed by the big company that now ran things. The tree-clad hills began to stretch bare and ruined as the ore was dug to feed the factories of the East. The river became heavily polluted and only Fern Creek stayed clear and sweet to supply the town with water. Piled-up spoil littered the area and a reddish dust settled on everything.

Murphy's Ford had been given a different name in the early days. It was then called Murphy's Crossing. But the copper mining had changed things. The level of the river dropped alarmingly as the polluted water was diverted. Folk were not going to pay when they could ride their wagons across the river or drive their cattle through it.

Only people without horses needed any sort of ferry, and there were few folk without horses in the township.

Shaun Murphy's son was left without a job. He found himself running a linen store and cursed the copper mining company that had reduced him to such degradation. The few remaining prospectors also cursed the miners. The creeks they had panned were now blocked with waste or buried by landslides.

But life was good for the rest of the inhabitants of Murphy's Ford. Most stores did a brisk trade. The old bank was pulled down and replaced by a new building of pale brick. There was the prospect of the railroad coming nearer if the town bribed the right people back East.

So it was that on a hot, sweaty afternoon, nobody paid much attention to a few strangers in Murphy's Ford. Three horsemen rode down the main street. They moved slowly and looked around with mild interest. Three more horsemen steered their mounts down a side lane where only the back doors of various buildings presented a cold aspect to anyone passing by. A solitary cat looked at the riders and went back to washing itself with a total lack of modesty.

One of the riders pulled his horse up at the back of the jailhouse. He dismounted and nodded to the others as he tried the door to quietly enter the building. His two companions rode on.

The intruder walked silently down the short corridor. There was a faint smell of coffee as he opened the door that gave on to the marshal's office. The lawman sat at the desk, his head sunk on his chest and a slight snore the only noise in the place.

A gun was drawn and placed firmly against the side of the marshal's head. He woke with a grunt.

'Just sit quiet-like,' the man told him. 'I ain't aimin' to kill you, but I sure as hell will if you as much as scratch your butt.'

Eli Riley was a big man with a weather-beaten face and blue eyes that radiated an honesty that everyone respected. He was a good marshal and his first thought was to buck the odds. But he was unarmed and the gun pressed against his unshaven cheek. He nodded and sat rigidly in the chair. His large hands rested on the desk as he looked longingly at his own holstered gun which hung on the rack near the carbines and shotguns that lined the opposite wall.

'What's all this about, fella?' he asked as calmly, as he could.

'We're robbin' your bank,' the man told him with a grin, 'and we don't figure on bein' disturbed by no lawman.'

'I got deputies. . . .'

'You got two and they're outa town lookin' for stray cattle.'

'You've done your scoutin' pretty well.' Eli Riley

snorted. 'Got somebody in town helpin' out?'

The man laughed. 'We don't need anybody,' he said smugly. 'My boss is a real professional. We rustled them cattle three days ago, and your bank is gonna be a pretty empty place in the next few minutes.'

The imposing building down the street contained two clerks, a manager, and three customers. It was an edifice as pompous as any that might be found in a bigger town. The long counter was highly polished and the copper oil lamps gleamed in their brass mounts. The overall effect was one of solid prosperity.

The three riders who had travelled along the main street pulled up at the hitching rail. They took a quick look round before entering the building. Their guns were ready as they confronted the two women customers and the elderly man who still had a wad of bank notes in his hand. The clerks did not hesitate to play safe. Their arms were in the air before the guns even pointed at them. A frightened silence reigned in the warmth of the building.

There were still the remaining two bank robbers who had ridden along the alley and were now at the back door of the bank. They looked around, but the only witnesses were scavenging birds. After dismounting one of them leaned over a fence and produced a large axe that had been hidden in a water trough. He shook it dry and grinned as he took one almighty swipe at the door. It gave way. The two men drew their guns and dashed into the short corridor. The manager's office was on their right and they burst in to confront the man who guarded the large safe and all its contents.

The frightened folk in the main part of the bank heard two loud explosions. They were shots from a heavy gun and the three bank robbers looked at each other in slight puzzlement. Then everything began to go wrong.

The door leading to the manager's office opened slowly. A man staggered out. He was clutching his chest and coughing blood as he stumbled towards one of the women customers. She screamed as he knocked her against the counter before collapsing. And then a figure appeared in the doorway like some avenging angel.

It was the manager. Leo Ramsay was of average height and weight, but dressed like some big town businessman. His cut-away coat and immaculate stock fitted perfectly. His watch chain was of heavy gold, and the pin that held his black neckwear in position was a golden horseshoe laced with diamonds. A handsome man of middle age, his really striking features were the splendid greying whiskers, which would have made the late General Burnside green with envy. And all was topped with a mass of wavy grey hair.

But nobody noticed any of these things. The two pistols that he held drew everybody's attention. And it was obvious that they had just been fired. The manager smiled broadly as he pointed the two cocked weapons at the remaining three robbers.

'Two dead, three to go, gentlemen,' he said in a calm voice. 'Folk don't rob this bank so easily.'

One of the bandits let out at a muttered curse and turned on his heel. He was out of the door before the others could stop him. Another of the hold-up men, a tall and hungry-looking fellow, decided to shoot it out. He swung his Colt .44 at the manager but Leo Ramsay was quicker. He pulled the trigger of the gun in his right hand and the man reeled back. He tried to raise his own pistol again but his hand shook and the weapon dropped to the floor. It seemed as though he were trying to reach the door, but he collapsed in a heap and lay moaning. The third man jumped over his comrade's body and wrenched at the large brass doorhandle to escape.

Another weapon roared in the confined space. A charge of buckshot caught the fleeing man and he crashed into the door before sliding to the ground amid a flurry of blood. There was a silence in the building as the smoke whirled around and the smell of burnt powder assailed the nostrils. The elderly clerk put the shotgun down on the counter and looked pleased with himself.

Nobody was as pleased as Leo Ramsay. The

11

moneylender stood puffing himself up with self-congratulation as he brandished the two old-fashioned Army Colts in his powder-stained hands.

'I reckon they won't be robbing any more banks,' he said, looking around for admiration.

He put the weapons down on the counter, gave a nod of approval to the clerk, and set about calming the two women. They soon succumbed to his expert charm while the male customer thankfully pocketed his own money and hurried to the saloon for something to settle his nerves before he told his tale.

'And where the hell is our marshal?' the bank manager asked rhetorically as he headed for the door. 'He'd have to be in the next county not to hear all the shooting.'

There was no sign of the lawman but a crowd now gathered noisily in front of the bank. They were all eager to report that one of the robbers had jumped on his horse and galloped wildly towards the southern end of the town. Eyes turned on the jailhouse, but the door did not open and the marshal's bay gelding stood patiently at the hitching rail. It appeared to be the only living thing not excited by what had happened.

It was the saloon owner who, having armed himself with a shotgun, crossed the street from the Golden Globe to confront the closed and locked door of the jailhouse. He pounded on it with the butt of the gun but nothing happened. A couple of other men ran round the corner to the alley. They found the back door open and fearfully entered the building. Marshal Riley was locked in his own cell and bombarding the air with an impolite opinion of bank robbers.

There were a lot of grinning townsfolk who led the embarrassed lawman to the front door of the bank where Leo Ramsay was holding forth to an admiring audience. Marshal Riley explained what had happened and took a quick look at the four dead or dying men. He pointed at the one who had staggered from the manager's office.

'Well, I don't know the others,' he said, 'but that's Fred Laver. There's a five-hundred-dollar reward for him. I reckon as how you'll be collectin' it, Leo.'

The manager beamed as the two men stepped over the body to get to his office. The man who had died there had already been removed and the stout doctor was fussing over the only living bank robber. He was the one who had been blasted by the shotgun. The medical man shook his head as he examined the damage that had been done.

When the door was closed and the two men had privacy, Leo Ramsay produced the whiskey and they sat down on opposite sides of his large desk. 'So what happened?' Eli Riley asked as he sipped the expensive branded liquor.

13

The bank manager grinned to display fine white teeth.

'I was sitting here as quiet as quiet could be,' he said almost as though he were rehearsing for future tales of heroism, 'and the alarm suddenly sounded.'

He pointed to a small bell that had been fixed on a bracket behind the door. A cord passed through the wooden wall into the main part of the bank.

'Old Simeon must have rung it when those three fellows entered the front door,' Leo explained. 'I knew that it meant trouble and I opened this drawer for my guns. Almost before I had time to get to my feet the rear door was smashed in and I had two more gunslingers right in my lap. But I was ready for them, Eli. Ready and willing to take on anybody who thought he could rob an old soldier. They just weren't expecting that and one was dead and the other dying before they knew what hit them.'

'I saw your guns on the counter,' Eli said with grudging admiration. 'You sure was takin' a risk with ancient things like that, Leo. And what in hell was a Southerner like you doin' with a coupla Bluebelly Colts anyway?'

The manager beamed. 'Captured them, I did, at Second Manassas,' he said modestly, 'and I've kept them loaded and cleaned ever since. They've got memories for me, Eli, and I'm proud to have found a use for them after all these years. You must come and see my collection of guns some time. Each one has a memory of things past and deeds done when we were fighting the Yankees.'

The marshal raised his glass and drank. He was trying not to smile at the self-satisfied look on the other man's face. Leo Ramsay had certainly been in the war, but the paymaster's staff were not famous for seeing action unless their own men rioted when the pay wagon did not turn up. Leo's heroic tales around town indicated that he had been a major. One or two of the old-timers who knew the facts had little doubt that he had never risen above the rank of top sergeant.

'You certainly did a good job, Leo,' the marshal assured him. 'I didn't come out so well, but I reckon as how you saved the bank one hell of a lotta cash.'

The manager leaned forward confidentially. 'We're holding close to twenty thousand dollars at present,' he said proudly. 'What with the copper company and the cattle sales last month, we're one hell of a prosperous outfit.'

'Well, I hope your bosses are grateful. I certainly am glad to be spared havin' to arrange trials for them fellas back there. The lawyers may be disappointed but you sure saved the town a bucketful of cash one way and another.'

'I did my duty.'

15

'You sure did, and now we can all settle down to a quiet life again. When word gets around, and it surely will, nobody's gonna cause trouble in Murphy's Ford.'

TWO

The man knelt at the side of the creek. He was stout and sweating under the hot sun. His clothes were dark and those of somebody more used to a town than to the wide expanse of dried grasses and tall cactus plants that surrounded him. A leather bag lay on the ground between him and the gurgling flow of clear water. Various bottles and jugs were scattered close by, and a small, leather-bound book was open on the gravelly soil.

He looked like some hard-selling whiskey drummer as he held up a small glass tube to the light and examined the liquid it contained.

A horse stood nearby in the shafts of a two-wheeled rig. It grazed mournfully on the stunted grass and swished its tail in a useless effort to fight off the flies. A jackrabbit watched from a distance, and so did a man who lay behind a jumble of rocks. He cradled an old Spencer rifle in his hands as he watched what was happening. Sweat dripped into his eyes and he dashed it angrily away with a

17

shake of the head. He levelled the gun and took careful aim at the kneeling man.

The crack of the gun was loud in the still air and the jackrabbit bolted for cover while several birds flew up from their insect-chasing and flapped wildly away. The kneeling man fell forward without a moan or a gesture of awareness. The glass tube dropped from his hand as he sprawled across the leather bag. The sound of breaking glass ended the silence that followed the shot. The gunman gave a slight smile and stood up. He tucked the rifle under his arm and came out from behind the rocks to go down the slope and look at the body. His victim was quite dead.

The killer picked up the leather bag and scattered glassware. He threw everything into a pile of mesquite and looked around to make sure that he had missed nothing. Then he dragged the heavy corpse to the rig and heaved it into the space below the seat. He gave the horse a sharp slap on the rump and stood grinning as it trotted thankfully away from the scene.

It was the middle of Sunday afternoon when a small rig entered the town of Murphy's Ford. It was drawn by a solitary horse that trotted gently down the main street. Somebody noticed the body lying prone across the space in front of the seat. There was a flurry of excitement as several men rushed to grab the animal and pull the little vehicle to a halt.

A woman called the marshal as the rig was led gently to his office halfway down the street. Eli Riley was a heavy man and the wooden boards of the stoop trembled beneath his feet as he came rushing out to see what was happening. He leaned into the rig and let out a loud curse as he recognized the man who lay there. One or two of the women, on their way home from Sunday meeting, looked shocked at his reaction. The majority of folk were more shocked when they realized that the dead man was their local doctor.

The marshal hesitated for a moment as he stared at the body. Then he recovered his poise and turned to one of his deputies.

'Take the rig to Will Brown's funeral parlour and get it unloaded round the back of the building. Tell Brown that I want the body left untouched until we can check on what happened.'

The deputy pointed to the wound in the back of the sagging corpse.

'He was shot, Marshal,' he explained patiently.

'I noticed that much, fella, but I need to know why, when, and how. I want the bullet for a start, and that means that we'll have to get Doc Morton out of the saloon to give us the benefit of his wisdom.'

'Is that possible?' the deputy asked doubtfully. 'He'll be on his way to fallin' over by this time of day.'

'It's Sunday and the saloon has only just opened.

19

With Doc Vale dead, he's the only medico we got. Sober the old fool up if you have to but get him to work. I want to know how long the doc's been dead. We sure got ourselves a bad one here. Who the hell would want to kill Doug Vale?'

The crowd heard his words and there were murmurings as they pushed each other to get a better view.

A slim man in a frock-coat and black stock had appeared on the scene. Folk made way for him and Mayor Hadley peered at the body as he wiped his brow with a large white bandanna. His thin hand shook as he turned away thankfully to take the marshal by the arm while the deputy and another man led off the rig.

'This is a terrible thing, Eli,' the mayor muttered as he tried to distance himself and the lawman from the crowd. The two men mounted the stoop again and entered the well-appointed jailhouse. The marshal produced a bottle of whiskey, the First Citizen took a glass gratefully and swallowed the contents in one gulp.

'Who's gonna tell Madge?' he asked fearfully.

The marshal refilled the glasses.

'I was hopin' you would,' he suggested. 'You bein' a friend of the family, as you might say.'

The mayor's hand started shaking again.

'Quite, quite, but she's a fearful woman,' he murmured. 'I'd rather try dealin' with the whole Apache nation. Perhaps the preacher could do it.

It's his sorta job when all's said and done.'

The marshal nodded agreement and the two men drank with a slightly lighter expression on their faces.

'But who in hell would want to kill Doug Vale?' the mayor muttered as he placed the glass hopefully on the desk.

The marshal shook his head. 'And to shoot him in the back,' he muttered angrily. 'I just don't figure it. And where the hell had he been at that time of day? I didn't see his doctorin' kit in the rig, and why go outa town on a Sunday?' He sighed. 'I suppose Madge will be able to tell us, when she's stopped shootin' up Murphy's Ford.'

'I'll go see the preacher,' the mayor volunteered. He headed for the door and then stopped as he opened it. 'We've no doctor now,' he murmured. 'What in blazes are we goin' to do?'

Eli Riley permitted himself a slight grin. 'There's always Jethro Morton,' he suggested.

The mayor shook his head in horror and left the office. The marshal put away the bottle and picked up his hat. He went out to the street and walked reluctantly down to the mortician's place of work. There were quite a few people gathered there and he hurried round to the rear door where his deputy stood guard. The lanky young man nodded to his boss and opened the door for him.

'I got Doc Morton here,' he said with a grin. 'He was at home and soon sobered up when I told him

21

that Doc Vale was dead.'

The marshal entered the dismal building and went reluctantly into the room where the dead man was laid out on a table. The gaunt mortician and a florid-faced doctor were standing in deep conversation and turned around as the lawman approached them.

'Got the bullet?' Eli Riley asked without looking at the body.

The doctor held it up. His hand was trembling slightly and his flushed face was wet with sweat.

'Why so much fuss about a bullet?' he asked.

The marshal took the small piece of lead and weighed it in his hand.

'This weren't fired from a pistol,' he said portentously. 'And it's one hell of a size for a bullet. Came from a rifle or a carbine. Maybe a Spencer or a Henry. And you don't see many of them about these days. All the fashion is for .44 Winchesters to match .44 pistols. So it might tell us somethin' about the killer. How long's he been dead, Doc?'

Jethro Morton looked at the mortician and then at the corpse on the table. His slightly unfocused eyes were baggy and watering.

'How the hell would I know?' he asked.

'You're a doctor is why.' The marshal's voice was impatient.

'Well, I ain't one of them investigatin' fellas,' the medico muttered, 'but I'd figure as how it happened a coupla hours ago. Killed on the spot, he was.'

'And from a distance,' the mortician added. 'No powder burns on his clothes.'

'I had noticed that,' the lawman said quietly.

Before anything more could be discussed the mayor came bustling in. He avoided looking at the body as he joined the little group.

'I've seen Preacher Edwards and he's gone to have a word with Ma Vale,' he said in a hoarse, almost reverent voice. 'The town's gonna want action on this, Eli. I sure hope you've got some ideas.'

'I ain't talked to his wife yet,' the marshal reminded him grimly. 'When the preacher's done his job, I'll be payin' her a call to find out where Doc Vale was goin' this morning. Until then, we just gotta wait.'

'There were stains on the knees of his pants,' the mortician said quietly.

They all turned to look at the tall, thin man with his grey face and silver-rimmed glasses.

'Water stains?' It was the marshal who asked.

'Just damp, as though he'd been kneelin' in grass with a little red dust mixed in. Funny thing he had in his pocket too.'

The mortician crossed the room to a roll-top desk. He picked up a small envelope of stiff brown paper and extracted some thin sheets.

'Test papers,' he pronounced. 'And what the

hell would he be doin' with them?'

The marshal took the little squares in his large hands and stared at them without understanding. They were of a delicate pink colour and looked almost transparent.

'And what are test papers?' he asked.

It was Doc Morton who answered.

'We were talkin' about them when you came in,' he explained. 'They're called litmus papers these days and doctors use them for checking on acids and alkalis. But we carry them in our bags, not loose like that. Doc Vale was a careful fella and I never reckoned as how he'd just throw a few in an envelope and carry them about on his travels. They could get contaminated.'

'But he didn't have his bag with him,' the marshal said slowly. 'Unless the killer took it.'

He handed the envelope back and stood looking silently at the dead man. Eli Riley was worried. Nothing made sense and he felt out of his depth.

'We'll just have to wait until I can talk to Ma Vale,' he said as he made to leave. 'She should know where the doc was headin' for. Maybe she'll tell the preacher and save me botherin' her.,

As if cued by some mysterious power, the deputy opened the door and ushered in the very man who was being mentioned. Preacher Edwards was small and stout, dressed in a neat black coat and waistcoat topped by a white shirt and black stock. A silver watch-chain shone across his ample belly as he hurried into the room.

'It's the most shocking thing I've ever seen in my life,' he moaned as he reached out with both hands as though seeking help. 'To be killed in such a frightful way.'

'He was just shot in the back,' the marshal said as kindly as he could. 'I don't reckon he felt a thing.'

'Oh, I don't mean Douglas Vale,' the preacher moaned as he headed for a cane chair and slumped into it. 'I mean Madge. She's been battered to death in her own home.'

THREE

Marshal Riley stood alone in the middle of the warm, sunlit room. Alone, save for the body of an elderly woman which lay on the floor between the large round dining table and the French harmonium. The place was spattered with blood from the wounds in her head and her grey hair had come loose from the pins that normally held it close in a tight bun.

The lawman had kept everybody else out until he could take stock of the situation. Eli Riley was a calm man who knew his job. But this was different. It was no ordinary shooting but savage blows with some weapon that was not visible. He checked the room for any sign of theft or damage. The others watched him from the doorway and he was conscious of a rising noise from the street.

The place seemed undisturbed and there was

even a purse on the table with several dollars in it alongside a bunch of keys. The marshal called to Doctor Morton and the mortician.

'You can get on with it now, fellas,' he said quietly. 'But try and tell me what sorta thing was used to kill her, if you can.'

The men came in and the doctor examined the body. Will Brown and his assistant prepared it for removal through the back door away from the avid curiosity of the noisy crowd. The mayor peered fearfully at the scene and grabbed the lawman by the arm.

'What's this all about, Eli?' he demanded uneasily. 'Two people killed in one day. And folk like the Vales. It don't make sense. Have we got some sort of madman loose in the town?'

The marshal did not answer. He walked along the corridor and opened the door of the late doctor's surgery. It was a small room with a large roll-top desk facing the window. There were papers on the floor and some of the drawers were still pulled out. A cardboard box-file lay on the desk, open and with some of its contents scattered around. The marshal looked at the glass-fronted medicine cabinet but it was locked and intact.

'It ain't no madman,' he muttered as he gazed around the little room. 'It's some fella with a real serious purpose. Any ideas, Mayor?'

Bert Hadley shook his head vigorously.

27

'I certainly haven't,' he sighed, 'but why kill Doc Vale and Madge? They never did harm to anyone, and she was the best nurse we ever had in Murphy's Ford. She was a bit of a terror, but folk could depend on her. I reckon she's delivered more babies than Wells Fargo has delivered freight. Why, in hell's name?'

'This place has been searched,' the marshal said as he pointed to the mess. 'And I reckon that whoever shot the doc came straight into town and called here. Ma Vale let him in and he clubbed her. Then he set about lookin' for somethin' and we don't know whether he found it or not.'

He turned to the deputy who stood in the door-way.

'Take over here, Ed,' he ordered, 'and when the doc and Will Brown are all done, lock up the house and go back to the office. I'm gonna have a word with Phineas Hoffman.'

The lanky deputy looked surprised.

'What's he got to do with it, Marshal?' he asked.

'He knows guns, lad. The bullet that killed Doc Vale ain't the sorta thing much used these days. I want to find out if any folk around here still buy bullets of that calibre. If anybody knows the answer to that, it'll be Phineas Hoffman.'

The gun store was at the far end of the street. It was just opposite the bank, with neat windows that sported a display of what was on offer inside.

Phineas Hoffman was a big man. Almost as tall

as the marshal, but running to fat and with a pasty, round face and wobbling chins. He greeted the lawman with a formal nod and examined the bullet he was shown with Germanic thoroughness.

'I'd say as how you will be lookin' for a Spencer rifle or carbine,' he said in his odd accent. 'This is a .56 calibre bullet and it would be in a rim-fire casing. Not many of them around these days. '

'Not since everybody wanted to match pistol and carbine ammunition,' the marshal said in an attempt to display his own knowledge.

The gunsmith nodded. 'A good weapon, but not used any more. Is this the bullet that killed Doc Vale?'

'Yes.'

The gunsmith put the little piece of lead on the glass-topped counter. He went to a shelf and took down a small packet of cartridges to show to the marshal.

'This is the only packet of .56 calibre I have in stock, and I haven't sold any of these for the last year or so.'

He opened the green-labelled pack of twenty and displayed the brass, rim-fire cartridges that sat snugly side by side. But three were missing. The two men looked at each other and the store owner turned the little cardboard box upside down to see if there was a hole through which the missing bullets could have escaped.

'How can that be?' he murmured. 'It was a full box and we don't sell odd bullets.'

'You ain't spilled them at some time, Phineas?'

'I'll swear I haven't. That box has just lain there for more than two years. I was hopin' that the fella who bought the other box would come back for more.'

'Who was the fella?' The marshal's voice was eager and tense.

The fat man shrugged his shoulders and his chins flopped around violently.

'I've no idea,' he admitted, 'but he does work for that copper minin' outfit. He comes into town regularly on one of their rigs and goes over to Will Penny's store. Buys all the sugar and coffee and other stuff for the mine.'

Eli Riley frowned. The copper mining company was a sensitive issue. If he told the mayor of his discovery, he would almost certainly be ordered to go easily. The town took too much money from doing business with the copper company, and the extension of the railroad line was dependent on their presence. The lawman thanked the gunsmith quietly and went back to the main street.

He walked slowly to the jailhouse and found his deputy making coffee.

'I got a little job for you, Ed,' he told him, 'but don't go at it like a lawyer after money. I want you to take a walk round the town and check every horse that's outside a saloon or store. Take a look in the livery stable as well. We're searchin' for a Spencer rifle or carbine in the saddle holster. Don't make it obvious and don't ask folk any questions. Just come back here and tell me if anythin' turns up.'

The young man hugged the coffee mug between his hands.

'I don't figure as I knows what a Spencer looks like, boss,' he said.

'I'm not so sure I do either.' The marshal grinned. 'But just tell me about anythin' unusual. It's possible that the fella what killed the doc is still in town. After all, he came into Murphy's Ford to kill Madge Vale. If he ain't got blood on him, he might just hang around for a while. If he'd gone gallopin' madly off after the killing, somebody might have spotted him. So just keep an eye on any strangers as well as lookin' for the Spencer.'

The young deputy finished his coffee and left the building in the gathering twilight. The marshal sat back in the chair. His arms were folded across his massive chest as he stared at the opposite wall. He felt like eating but his long-suffering wife would have to wait until he had thought over the events of the day.

He needed to talk to somebody and eventually he got to his feet to go along to the mayor's office. Bert Hadley ran a feed store behind the main

31

street and his place of work was a small wooden building above the granary. He also owned the proudly named Hadley House Hotel. It was run by his only son and the family lived at the rear of the well-furnished building.

A flight of rickety wooden steps led up to the office and the marshal could see that a light burned behind the small window. At least the First Citizen was still putting in a few hours'work and probably felt as worried as the lawman.

Eli Riley was greeted with a welcome that was almost a gesture of relief on the mayor's part. The two men sat opposite each other at the large desk and glasses of whiskey were poured.

'I been thinkin' about this thing,' the marshal said slowly.

The mayor nodded eagerly. 'Me too, Eli. It's somethin' right outside my experience. Got any ideas?'

'Well, Phineas Hoffman agrees with me about the bullet that killed Doug Vale. He thinks it comes from an old Spencer rifle or carbine. But then we get into deep water.'

He told the mayor about the missing bullets and the box of cartridges that were bought by an employee of the copper company. Mayor Hadley shook his head violently.

'We can't go makin' trouble for them,' he whined. 'You gotta go careful thcre, Eli. Them minin' folk is just about keepin' this town goin' strong. Anyway, why should one of them kill the doc and his wife?'

'Oh, I aim to go quietly about things,' the marshal assured him in a pacifying voice. 'And somethin' has occured to me that makes it unlikely that the copper fellas were mixed up in this, y'see, most of the workers out at the mines don't have horses. They come into town on the wagons when they're paid. I figure that we're dealin' with a fella that uses a horse and would be able to ride in and out of Murphy's Ford without bein' noticed.'

The mayor nodded happy agreement. 'A ranch hand or some other local fella,' he suggested.

'Yeah, more likely. Most of them minin' fellas is foreigners and don't even carry guns. The bullets missing from the box could just have got tipped out accidental-like. They might have been stolen while he was back in the workshop. Phineas Hoffman don't have nobody workin' for him, so I figure he can't have his eye on the customers all the time.'

The marshal sat quietly for a moment, then, since the mayor did not seem disposed to hand out another drink, he finally rose to leave.

'I'd sure like to find out where Doc Vale had been, though,' he said sorrowfully.

The mayor shrugged. 'I guess we'll never know,' he muttered. 'He was certainly with Madge at the prayer meetin' this morning.'

Eli Riley left soon afterwards and walked back towards his jailhouse. It was dark now and the lights were on in the windows along the main street. He decided to go into the Golden Globe saloon and have a word with Doc Morton. It could just be that the two medical men had exchanged a few confidences that might help. The noisy drinking place was quite full. It was the better of the two saloons and one customer had sat down at the piano and was hammering out something that seemed quite tuneless to the ears of the lawman.

Heads turned at the sight of the marshal as he looked around at all the familiar faces. Doc Morton was not among them, and that was unusual for such a dedicated drinker. Eli left the place thoughtfully and walked slowly down a lane that led to the house and surgery of the only remaining medical man in Murphy's Ford. There was a light in one of the lower windows and he knocked loudly on the heavy door.

'Who's there?' The voice was scared and hoarse.

Eli identified himself. After some delay he heard the drawing back of the bolts. The doctor ushered him into the house and the lawman noticed that there was a shotgun leaning against the wall just inside the door.

'You ain't very welcoming, Doc,' he said as he nodded at the weapon. 'If I didn't know better, I'd take you for one very scared man.'

'I'm just bein' careful, Eli,' Jethro Morton said

as he led the way through to the living room. It was a dismal place with only one oil lamp lit and looked dank and untidy. His wife had walked out several years earlier and the doctor's habits did not include cleaning a house. The two men sat down in dust-covered armchairs.

'I thought I'd see you over at the saloon, Doc,' Eli said as he looked around.

The other man did not answer right away. He sat crouched in the chair with restless hands trembling on his knees. His usually high colour seemed to have faded and the marshal knew that he was looking at somebody who was very frightened.

'What's worryin' you, Jethro?' he asked in a reassuring voice. 'I'm here to help.'

The medico snorted impatiently.

'How the hell can you help? Doug Vale and his wife are dead, and you've got two useless deputies pushed on to you by the councilmen. One of them isn't even in town right now. I ain't sayin' they're bad fellas, Eli, but they're both tied up with the folks that run this town. They're all kin to one another.'

Eli Riley frowned. He had no way of rebutting what the doctor was saying.

'And you think someone's out to kill you?' he asked in wonder. 'Why should that happen? What do you think is happenin' around here, Doc?'

Then his eye caught sight of a carpetbag that lay under the round mahogany table. It was a large one and bulged with its heavy load.

'Goin' somewhere, Doc?' he asked.

'I sure as hell am goin' somewhere. I'm gettin' outa this town before the copper company does to me what they've already done to the Vales. That's what it's all about, Eli. Them minin' fellas are poisonin' Murphy's Ford.'

FOUR

There was a long and uncomfortable silence. Eli Riley looked round the untidy room and eventually spotted a whiskey bottle and a couple of reasonably clean glasses on top of a cupboard. He rose and helped himself to a drink.

'Do you want one as well?' he asked.

The doctor shook his head. 'No, I'm right sober this night, Eli,' he said grimly, 'and I don't aim to take another drink until I feel one hell of a lot safer than I do now.'

'I think as you must have a lot to tell me, Jethro,' the lawman said as he sat down again. 'After all, we've had two killings and I'm supposed to be the law around here. Suppose you let me have the full story.'

Doc Morton heaved a heavy sigh and clutched the arms of the chair with large-veined hands.

'Doc Vale came to see me a few weeks ago. Just before that bank raid, it was,' he said quietly. 'I was in the saloon as usual and he took me across to his place where we could talk private-like. He said that he'd had a few kids and some old folks taken ill with some sort of stomach trouble. None of them was in danger but they was all real upset. The kids was off school and the old people was laid up in their beds. Now I ain't got many patients these days, but I did recall that three of mine had the same symptons. We talked about it, or at least he did. But I didn't reckon at the time that it was anythin' out of the ordinary. Meat and fish go off in this hot weather and folk ain't always careful.'

He licked his lips and looked longingly at the whiskey bottle. After a determined fight against temptation, he continued:

'Then he told me that folks usin' wells for their water supply seemed to be safe. It was the ones that used Fern Creek who was sufferin' with their stomachs. My three patients used water from the creek. I gotta admit that at that point I began to take him seriously. He'd ridden out to the creek and found that a lot of waste from the mine was bein' blown into the northern, fast-movin' stretch by the winds comin' off the hills. He couldn't be sure about it but he went along to the office of the minin' company and saw their big chief.'

'Ross Kimber?'

'The boss man himself. Kimber told Doug that they had their own people checkin' the water. He said that no traces of copper ever got into the town supply. The dust was heavy, he admitted, but it soon settled on the bottom just like any other wind-blown dirt.'

The doctor eyed the whiskey again and licked his lips.

'He was real nasty about it,' he went on, 'and Doug Vale told me that he felt mighty scared of bein' out there alone. He decided to go back again and check on the water with chemicals and such-like. He started talkin' real scientific stuff. He even sent for a book and some other gear, and when it came in on the freight line he read up on the subject and then said he felt he knew enough to go out and test the creek. Well, we all know what happened to him.'

'So why are you runnin' scared, Doc?'

Jethro Morton shifted uneasily in his chair.

'Doug Vale and I talked quite a few times,' he said tremulously, 'and folks must have noticed how friendly we suddenly were. After all, he'd never been on what you might call visitin' terms with a fella like me. And our meetings start just when he's gettin' interested in the minin' company. And they're private meetings we're having, I figured as how somebody might think I knew too much. That minin' company's got plenty of friends in this town.'

Eli Riley poured himself another drink. He noticed for the first time that an uneaten meal of bread and bacon sat on the table alongside a cold cup of coffee.

39

'Did Doc Vale talk to the mayor or any of the councilmen?' he asked.

'I don't know. He said as how they was all in the pockets of the minin' company. Those folks bring big money to Murphy's Ford and they're never tired of tellin' us that we owe the nearness of the railroad to them. I've heard tell that the mayor and a few others get a regular supply of dollars for not listenin' to complaints.'

The marshal nodded reluctantly. 'And there surely have been complaints,' he admitted slowly. 'The goldminers reckon as how the company are on land where they might have made claims. And the ranchers ain't too pleased up Broughton way.'

'If that were all, Eli. Those homesteaders along the heights are seeing trees bein' pulled down. They're losin' the timber they need and there's nothin' they can do about it. And it's gonna get worse. The company are bringin' in steam shovels.'

Eli Riley's glass stopped halfway to his lips.

'And what the hell would they be?' he asked.

'They're mechanical scoops that move more earth in a day than an army of workmen could do in a week. They're gonna be used along Flint Ridge and down Colton way. All that scrub and grazin' will go, and they've got backin' from Washington and all the folks who make money out of the deal. The mayor knows that in a year or so, this town could be the richest in the territory. He

40

ain't gonna raise a finger to stop the copper minin' fellas. He's figurin' that if he plays along, the railroad will come right into town and he'll be the local hero.'

Eli Riley sat silently for a while. He knew the attitude of the local businessmen and politicians. They kept him away from meetings of the council and often stopped talking when he approached a group of them. His two deputies had not been picked by him. They were related to local worthies and could not be trusted to keep their mouths shut about the activities of the marshal's office.

'Well, I guess you know what's best for you, Doc,' he said eventually. 'But this town needs you right now, and if you can lay off the firewater you could enjoy one hell of a livin' here in Murphy's Ford.'

The medical man smiled grimly. 'If I lived long enough to enjoy it,' he said quietly. 'I'd be gettin' all Doug Vale's patients, and that includes those poisoned by this copper business. What would I do then? Where would I get help? Mayor Hadley and the rest would probably run me outa town for creatin' a fuss. If the copper fellas didn't get me first. Your own position ain't too good either, Eli. Have you thought about that? If you pin these two killin's down to the minin' company, where the hell will that leave you? You really think the town will be on your side?'

The marshal swallowed noisily. 'The ordinary

folk will be,' he said uncertainly. 'The Vales were popular.'

'Ordinary folk don't count, Eli. This town would have a new marshal before you could scratch your butt.'

The lawman said nothing but he knew that the man was speaking the truth. He rose to leave, feeling defeated and unsure what action to take next. It was the doctor who suddenly spoke in a slightly firmer voice.

'I suppose you know that the Vales have a son,' he said with a raise of his eyebrows. 'He should be comin' into Murphy's Ford any day now.'

Eli Riley stopped in his tracks.

'No, I didn't know of any kin,' he admitted. 'Has he been told about his folks?'

'Preacher Edwards went to the telegraph office earlier today. That son will be wantin' justice to be done. He'd be a handy man to have on your side, Eli.'

There was a long silence and the lawman looked carefully at the doctor as he noted the expression on the man's face.

'Are you tryin' to tell me something, Jethro?' he asked.

'Ever heard of Tom Vale?' the doctor asked.

'Sure, but – I never thought to connect him with the doc.' Marshal Riley shook his head in bewilderment. He had heard of Tom Vale as had quite a lot of lawmen. And heard nothing good.

'So he's Doc Vale's son,' he muttered. 'That sure takes some beating.'

'He'd be useful in a fight,' the medico said slyly.

'Yeah, I reckon he would at that, but he ain't a fella with much respect for the law. You've heard about his wanderings, I take it?'

'Doug Vale told me. But he's honest in his beliefs, and if he don't have respect for the law, it could be that the law sometimes gets it all wrong. Lawyers and politicians make law, Eli. They make it for themselves, not for ordinary folks like you and me. Tom Vale believes in justice, and that ain't the same thing as law. Not in this territory, anyways.'

'He was slung out by the Pinkerton people too,' the marshal pointed out grimly. 'Then he worked as a deputy with the Earps in Tombstone. They dropped him like a hot horseshoe within the year. He seems to have hired himself out as a gun after that. This town won't take kindly to his arrival.'

The doctor managed a slight grin. 'I'd like to be here when he does turn up,' he said. 'All them crooked fellas round the mayor will start wonderin' if he's diggin' into their affairs. I might not be the only one leavin' town in a hurry.'

FIVE

Eli Riley watched the doctor board his small rig and whip the horse to a rapid pace to disappear into the darkness on the outskirts of town. Then the marshal went along to the house of Doctor and Mrs Vale to have another look around without being pestered by people like the mayor and the judge. He lit a couple of oil lamps and wandered from room to room. His search was a bit aimless in view of the fact that he did not really know what he was looking for.

He soon gave up, locked the house carefully and returned to his office. His other deputy was back in town and the marshal sent both men on patrol near the two saloons. He did not want any drunken disturbances to add to his woes. The truth was that Eli Riley felt completely out of his depth. The attempt at robbing the bank a few weeks earlier still rankled. And now he had two prominent citizens killed right under his nose.

He sat down at his desk and looked despairingly

across the office at nothing in particular. His fingers tapped restlessly on the woodwork as he tried to make up his mind about the happenings of the day. The sudden opening of the outer door brought him back to reality as the mayor entered in a flurry of excitement.

'What the hell is all this about Doc Morton leavin' town?' the First Citizen barked angrily. 'Word is all round the Golden Globe that the old drunk lit out like all hellfire was on his tail. And folks is sayin' that you helped him get his rig harnessed and then saw him off.'

The marshal suppressed a grin. 'He's scared of bein' killed,' he said bluntly, 'and he's been tellin' me tales that leave the copper minin' fellas lookin' real guilty.'

The mayor seemed to freeze. 'What's this all about?' he asked in a quieter voice. 'I'm runnin' this town, Eli, and I have a right to know. You were sayin' it was some local fella a few hours ago.'

He sat down at the desk and wiped his face with a large white bandanna.

The marshal told him what the doctor had said and Bert Hadley listened in growing horror. He shook his head occasionally and the marshal took pity on the man sufficiently to pour him a glass of whiskey.

'I just don't believe any of this,' the mayor said as he sipped thankfully. 'These minin' fellas are responsible folk and they're good to this town.

They don't go around shootin' like that and batterin' women to death.'

The marshal was beginning to enjoy himself for the first time that day.

'There's a fella up at the mines called Frank Hayden,' he said slowly. 'The bosses brought him in when the workers put down tools and walked out last year. You remember?'

The mayor nodded impatiently. 'Yes, yes. They wanted more money and shorter hours,' he said. 'So, what's this Hayden fella got to do with things?'

'He's a hired gun. The bosses of the minin' company had him work over a few of the leaders. It soon brought them into line and they've had no trouble since. But he's been kept on, and he's the sorta fella who would be likely to kill the doc and Ma Vale if the money was right. He'll do any dirty work these responsible businessmen would want doin' without soilin' their own fair hands.'

'Oh, I don't believe that for a moment. Look, Eli, I know that you want to clear up this business, but the good of the town has to come first. Folk here are dependin' on the copper mines. Our whole future is tied up with these people. Now, I ain't sayin' as how they may or may not have damaged the water supply accidental-like, but we've got to be understandin' and take things gently.'

'You want that I should stay away from them and not ask any awkward questions, then?'

46

The mayor avoided the marshal's cynical expression.

'Well, not exactly. But the truth is that I've been havin' talks with some of the councilmen tonight. They all feel that you might go at this thing like a mad coyote in a hencoop.'

The marshal grinned broadly. 'Well, it's certainly true that I might ask some nasty questions. But it might be as well for your councilmen to remember that there are some folks in Murphy's Ford whose kids are pretty sick right now.'

'All that will pass, Eli. None of the kids is in any danger. But this town is. And just remember that we are goin' to need the minin' folk until we can get ourselves another doctor. I'm goin' to have to go up there and ask Ross Kimber if his medical fella will come into town now and then to help us out. I can hardly do that if the marshal is makin' trouble. Now can I?'

'These council fellas you've been talkin' to,' the marshal said with heavy sarcasm, 'was the preacher among them? Or Peter Murphy who has two sick girls and a hell of a hot temper? Remember that Murphy carries a lot of weight with ordinary folk. His pa founded this place.'

'The Reverend Edwards isn't a councillor,' the mayor snapped. 'And we don't take no heed of a hot-headed drunk who bears a grudge because he's failed in life.'

The marshal put away the whiskey bottle as a certain sign that the pleasantries were over.

'You gotta face facts, Bert,' he said in a low voice. 'Word is goin' around town faster than water through a faucet. Folk will want somethin' done about what's been happenin' here. They'll be thinkin' more of their kids and their safety than of Murphy's Ford and the welfare of councilmen on the minin' company's payroll. They might even be wantin' a new mayor unless they get action. That's when they've lynched the old one, of course. Think hard about it, Bert. You can always get rid of me and let one of my deputies play at bein' a lawman. But if you wanta survive, you gotta find out who killed the Vales.'

The mayor shook his head with apparent sadness.

'You must understand, Eli,' he said earnestly, 'that the whole town is lookin' to me. We had that bank hold-up a few weeks ago and you ended up in your own cell. It was Leo Ramsay who saved the situation. Now we got two killings and folk is goin' to want real action. But they won't want you blamin' the minin' company. Maybe you should consider retirin' to that ranch your son has down South. I reckon the town could pay you a decent amount of money to start a new life there.'

He looked hopefully at the marshal and his tone was almost imploring. There was a long silence before Eli Riley spoke. Then he stood up and towered over the seated mayor.

'Have you seen Phineas Hoffman tonight?' he asked.

'No. Why?'

The marshal nearly managed a smile. 'Phineas Hoffman is an honest man, Bert,' he said slowly, 'and as I told you earlier, he knows about that bullet. Now he ain't gonna keep it quiet. The minin' company don't mean a thing to a man like him. If he relied on their trade, he'd be out of business tomorrow. He's gonna talk to folks, Bert, and they'll listen to him.'

The mayor's tongue ran uneasily round his dry lips. 'We've got to do somethin' about all this, Eli,' he muttered, 'but I don't want this town harmed.'

'So what do you suggest I do?'

'I'll – I'll leave that to you, but don't do anythin' that will get us in bad with the copper company.'

The marshal knew that he had won and decided to take some pity on the sweating politician.

'Lookit, Bert,' he said kindly, 'I'll try and trace this Spencer rifle first of all. The deputies are out there tryin' to do that right now. And I'll tell you somethin' else. I ain't blamin' the minin' company at present. The fella who came into town and stopped at the food store was gettin' on in years. He don't sound to me like the type who would be goin' around shootin' folks. And a real professional gunslinger would be usin' a Winchester sure as sure. The killer came into town after shootin' the doc. Does that sound like somebody from the mine? He'd have stood out like an Apache brave at that time of day.'

The marshal scratched his chin thoughtfully.

'He had to be someone who could call on Ma Vale and get into her house,' he went on. 'He killed her without a struggle. Now, I ain't no Pinkerton agent, but I've had a good look round her place tonight. She weren't attacked near the door. It was somebody she knew and took through to the living room.'

The mayor began to cheer up. 'I hope you're on the right track, Eli,' he said, 'but there's got to be some fast action to satisfy folks that we're doin' somethin' about this trouble.'

'Just leave it with me for a day or so, Bert.'

The mayor nodded and turned to go. Eli Riley let him get to the door before delivering his final touch of mischief.

'Doc Vale had a son,' he said quietly. 'He'll be comin' into town any day now.'

The mayor nodded sadly.

'Yes, the Reverend Edwards told me that he'd sent a message to the young fella. Seems he went East for a good education. He might even be a medical man. That would certainly solve one of our problems, wouldn't it?'

'It would,' the marshal grinned. 'But he never did get around to studyin' medicine so far as I know, Bert. He took up gunslingin' instead. And I figure as how he'll be on the prod when he reaches Murphy's Ford and hears all the details.'

The mayor stopped in his tracks with a hand on the half-open door.

'You'll have to keep an eye on him then,' he said sharply. 'I don't want any more shootin' round the town.'

'I can only do that if I'm still the marshal.'

There was a long silence until the mayor nodded his head in dumb agreement before leaving the office. The lawman crossed to the window and looked out on the main street. It was near to midnight and the Golden Globe was beginning to shed the drinkers as they made their ways noisily to their homes. The other saloon was out of sight in one of the side lanes. It was a cheaper and rowdier place with high wines pretending to be whiskey and beer that was watered down.

Eli Riley felt that he needed a glass of beer himself. He was not really a whiskey drinker and what he had sipped with the mayor had made his mouth dry. He heaved a sigh and sat down at the desk. There was little hope of his deputies finding a gun.

He had dozed a little when the door opened and let in a blast of night air. The marshal tried to appear as if he had been doing something useful but relaxed when he saw that it was one of his deputies.

Ed Taylor was tall and gangly and seemed to fall

into the jailhouse as he made his report.

'We got trouble, Marshal,' he panted. 'Word has got around about that Spencer rifle and the fella from the copper company what had it. He's in the Palomino saloon right now and folks there is gettin' real edgy. The only thing savin' him is that he's got about half a dozen other company men with him.'

'Is the rifle there as well?' Eli asked urgently as he got up and began to buckle on his gun belt.

'We ain't looked yet. His wagon is outside the Palomino and I reckon as how he brought some of the workers into town for a drink. It was Phineas Hoffman what knew him. Word went round like forked lightnin' and I've left Sid to keep an eye on things while I reported back here. I don't know if he can hold them. The mood is sure gettin' ripe for a lynchin' party.'

The marshal took down a shotgun and motioned his deputy to do the same.

'Come on, lad,' he growled. 'I don't aim to have a lynchin' in my town. I've got enough troubles.'

The two men set out to walk the length of the main street and then head down a lane for the wilder of the two saloons.

They were too late. A fight had already broken out between the copper workers and the town folks. It could be heard by the two lawmen before they even got a sight of what was happening. The copper workers were grouped round their elderly wagon driver and had steered him out to the street. He was already injured by someone's fist and needed helping on to the seat of the wagon. The others climbed aboard, fighting off their opponents with fists or boots as they helped the old man gather up the reins and whip the two horses into action.

The wagon sprang forward and knocked down several men who tried to grab the headbands of the animals. The driver lashed out with his whip and caught another one who attempted to scramble on to the seat. Somebody pulled a gun and a shot echoed round the town as one of the mine workers stumbled from the rig and sprawled on the dry ruts of the dusty street.

A shout of triumph went up but the wagon was now well under way. It careered along the street, past the approaching lawmen, and began to turn at the corner that would lead it through the cattle pens to the edge of town. Then another shot was fired. One of the horses stumbled. The other animal bumped into it, sawed at the reins and veered into the wooden post of a hitching rail. The wheels of the wagon mounted the steps of the bootmaker's store and the rig began to overturn.

It all seemed to happen in slow motion and the pursuing town folk stopped in their tracks to watch. Some of the copper men jumped clear as the whole thing fell on its side and the elderly driver lay trapped between the edge of the seat and the hard ground. It was all over and there would be no need for a lynching.

Something had fallen clear of the wreckage. It was a Spencer carbine that had been tucked away under the driver's seat. One of the townsmen held it up and gave a shout of triumph. It was the other deputy who now intervened. He snatched the gun from the jubilant attacker and took it across to the approaching marshal as though he had been the one who discovered it. Eli Riley took it from him and turned the heavy weapon over in his large hands. He looked around at the mass of slightly drunken faces until he found the one he was looking for.

Phineas Hoffman was big enough to stand apart from the rest of the crowd and the marshal went across and thrust the gun into his hands.

'Let's go back to your store, Phineas,' he said tersely, 'and check this gun over. I want to know if it's the one that killed Doc Vale.'

The large gunsmith was looking a little sheepish. He led the way back to the main street, the weapon held like a baby in his stout arms. The rest of the town seemed to be following and they crowded on to the wooden stoop and out into the street as he unlocked his door.

It took a few minutes to light the large oil lamps and bring one to the glass-topped counter. A mirror was placed behind it to give more light and the gunsmith put on a pair of gold-rimmed glasses after he had laid the gun on a sheet of green baize.

One of the deputies had closed the door but the mob could still be heard as they tried to look in at the windows. Phineas took his time. His hands were steady as he checked every detail of the heavy weapon.

'It's the right calibre,' he pronounced at last, 'but this old thing has not been fired in a coon's age.'

SIX

It took some time to get Murphy's Ford back to
normality. The joint funerals of Doc Vale and his
wife were attended by most of the townsfolk. The
preacher spoke out with his usual bluntness and
honesty. He mentioned the fouling of the water
supply, dwelt long and loudly on the death of the
old wagon driver, and stared out at the bowed
heads of his shamed listeners.

The mayor sat uneasily on the front row. He
looked a worried man who had not stored up
enough courage to ride out to the copper mine to
tender his regrets for what had happened. He had
at least sent a note and quickly replaced the
damaged wagon. He had also watched fearfully as
the angry miners drove out with their wounded
comrade next to the corpse of the man who had
owned the Spencer carbine. That had also been
sent back. It was an old and rusted weapon covered
in the dust of ages and probably a bigger danger to

whoever pulled the trigger than to the intended victim.

It was three days after the funeral that things began to happen. A solitary figure rode into town one morning. He was a tall, thin man with a narrow, dark face and eyes that appeared to assess keenly and challenge everything they saw. Danger seemed to be written all over him and the two guns at his belt gave ample warning of his trade. He was dressed in dark clothes and travelled on a large black gelding that bore a saddle holster bearing a Winchester carbine. The calibre matched that of the Colts at his waist.

People stared but nobody dared to challenge him. One of the deputies was sitting on the porch of the jailhouse. He suddenly decided to go inside rather than risk being approached by the stranger. He told Marshal Riley what he had seen and the lawman crossed to the window.

'It's Frank Hayden,' Eli Riley quietly murmured. He breathed a sigh of relief as the man rode past the jailhouse and headed for the residence of the mayor. The Hadley House hotel was the best in town and was furnished with goods from the East. It smelled clean and had well-trained staff who looked after the richer visitors to Murphy's Ford. The mayor played no part in the management but left it all to his son. Young Jim Hadley was an enigmatic character with a shrewd head for business and an eye for a quick dollar. The mayor lived at the back of the building with his stout wife.

'I reckon as how that's one visitor who won't be gettin' a warm welcome,' the marshal chuckled. 'Your uncle Bert is in for a mighty unpleasant experience, lad.'

Young Ed licked his lips.

'What are we gonna do, Marshal?' he asked uneasily.

The lawman thought for a moment. His grin was reflected in the window through which he looked.

'Well, I fancy goin' down to Ma Fitton's place for a cup of decent coffee and a slice of her mutton pie. Where's Sid?'

'He's brushin' down the horses.'

'Then go help him saddle them and you can both ride out and have a word with Will Brewster about that drunk that keeps raidin' his stock.'

The young deputy gave a relieved and toothy smile. He was out of the back door before the marshal could change his mind.

Mayor Hadley was looking through the books in the hotel office when the door burst open. He looked up from the ledgers and paled visibly as he saw the tall, slim figure of Frank Hayden.

'Your name Hadley?' the man asked in a quiet voice.

The First Citizen nodded silently. His mouth was too dry to utter words.

'Mr Kimber ain't pleased with what's been

58

happenin' in this town,' the man went on. 'Your folks have killed old Steve Kellerman. They've wounded one of our foremen, wrecked a wagon, and injured a good horse.'

'I did write an apology,' the mayor managed to stutter, 'and I sent another wagon and horse.'

'An old rig that's still got the brand of a Yankee regiment burned into its ass. And a horse that's blind in one eye. You're one mean-spirited fella, Mr Mayor, and my boss reckons as how you owe him money.'

The mayor relaxed a little. If his life was not under threat and they were talking cash, he was back on safer ground. He waved the man to a seat at the other side of the desk and leaned forward with an ingratiating smile.

'I can't argue with that,' he said with apparent frankness. 'What does Ross Kimber reckon would settle matters?'

'Old Steve Kellerman had a wife and daughter. That'll cost this town two hundred dollars. There's another forty dollars for the rig and thirty dollars for the horse. The fella what got wounded figures to settle for thirty dollars. That comes to a nice round three hundred. Pay that into the bank and the boss will say no more. '

'It's rather a lot,' the mayor suggested tentatively. 'The councilmen might not agree.'

'If they wanta keep drawin' prizes outa the cracker barrel, they'd better agree. You just put it to them, Mr Mayor. And if any of them do get a bit uppity, tell them I'll pay them a call and explain things in easier ways.'

His hand tapped one of the guns at his side and the dry face almost smiled.

Mayor Hadley nodded dumbly. He made no attempt to move as the visitor stood up and turned to leave the office. Frank Hayden closed the door behind him and walked through the carpeted foyer to the wooden porch of the hotel. Two of the guests sat in wicker chairs on the stoop but it was not they who drew the gunslinger's attention. A group of at least a dozen men stood in the street, and all of them were armed.

He stopped in the doorway, his hand going automatically for the Colt at his right side. As his fingers curled round the butt, a hail of shotgun blasts split the air. The windows of the hotel were shattered and Frank Hayden staggered backwards against the wall. His right arm was broken and he tried pulling the other gun as he lurched around in an attempt to stay on his feet. The shotguns deafened the ears again as the triumphant towns-folk closed in on their victim. The gunslinger collapsed on the wooden boards. A partly drawn Colt slithered out of the holster and the dying man rolled over a few times before lying still in the open doorway.

Both the visitors had been hit by stray buckshot and dashed into the building for help. The mayor did not appear. He was too experienced to put himself in danger and sat at the desk as though in a trance. It was the linen-store owner who came out from behind the grinning group of men that crowded round the corpse. Peter Murphy had seen the visitor enter the hotel and had quietly slipped away to collect a few of the men whose children, like his own, were ill from the water infection. They had been only too willing to help rid the town of copper miners and their gunslingers.

The marshal arrived, clutching his mutton pie and not appearing to be very concerned at what had happened. He stood quietly while the mortician came gleefully to take charge and ask if the town was paying the bill. Mayor Hadley eventually decided to put in an appearance and stepped cautiously over the bloodied corpse. He surveyed the ruined windows and scarred door with obvious dismay. His son was at his side, silent and watchful.

'You didn't have to do this,' the mayor told the crowd sadly. 'He wasn't threatenin' me and we'd come to an agreement.'

It was Peter Murphy who spoke up.

'Did you come to an agreement about poisonin' our kids?' he bawled. 'That fella was the hired gun what killed the doc and his wife.'

There was a loud chorus of support and the mayor looked to the marshal for help.

'Just break it up,' Eli Riley told them firmly. 'I

reckon that you'll all be tellin' me that this fella drew first and was in town to make trouble. So just go your ways while I still believe that story.'

There was no argument and the grinning men went along to the Palomino saloon to celebrate their bravery. Young Tom Hadley stood at his father's side while the mayor approached the marshal. Eli Riley still held his mutton pie and grinned amiably as he listened to Bert Hadley complaining about the damage to his property, the rupture of good terms with the copper company, and the absence of law when it was needed.

'My deputies had to ride out to Brewster's place,' the marshal explained calmly, 'and I'd gone along to Ma Fitton for a mutton pie. A fella has to eat.'

'A mutton pie! For God's sake, Eli, this is a cow town!' the mayor shrieked.

'That's why a bit of mutton makes a welcome change. Now, suppose you tell me what Frank Hayden wanted.'

The mayor explained and the marshal listened quietly. He noted that the bewhiskered bank manager and the owner of the Golden Globe saloon were approaching. Both were councilmen and as worried about the situation as the mayor.

The lawman left them to it and retired to his office to finish the pie and have another cup of his own over-stewed coffee. He had been thinking things over and come to the conclusion that there was a little journey he had to make in the next day or two.

SEVEN

There was a low, damp mist over the creek. The distant hills were blotted out and a dull sky added to the gloom that Marshal Riley felt as he rode slowly along the edge of the water.

He was scanning the ground carefully for any sign of a rig and horses. His eyes were watering in the sharpness of the cold early morning and he guessed that he might have to travel several miles along the creek until he found any clue to what the doctor had been doing when he was killed.

His reasoning was that the medical man would have chosen a place well out of town and yet clear of the copper mining area. He would not want to be seen while he checked the water. Yet somebody had seen him. Somebody had either come from the mines or had followed him from town. Eli Riley still favoured a killer from Murphy's Ford. It seemed more likely. Somebody who supported the company and did not want any pollution found that could be nailed down to their activities. If that was the case, then it had all gone wrong for the killer. The doctor had talked to his medical colleague and the whole town was now in arms against the copper mines.

The marshal smiled as he rode. It gave him a certain pleasure to picture the dismay of the banker and the mayor that any trouble might bring. They and all their business friends were well and truly in the pocket of Ross Kimber. And the extension of the railroad right into town was Bert Hadley's big dream. It might even get him elected to the territorial legislature.

By the time the sun warmed up the atmosphere, Eli Riley had covered some twelve miles or more. He had seen nothing save for a few animals and flocks of birds that rose from his path. He was thirsty and hungry, and beginning to sweat and felt tired. Then he saw something ahead that made him draw on the reins as he steered his horse into the shelter of a clump of tall mesquite to the right of the trail. He dismounted quietly and tethered the animal to some of the lower branches. The Winchester was taken from the saddle holster and he checked its load before moving off on foot towards what had caught his attention.

A mule grazed quietly by the creek. Its rear feet were in the cool water as it chewed on the succulent grasses on the bank. A man sat beneath the shade of some brambles while the smoke from his clay pipe and cooking fire drifted up on the still air. He was an old-timer, with a rough grey beard and tanned face that was as wrinkled as the filthy old hat that rested low on his brow. The marshal drew a sigh of relief as he advanced towards the lone figure.

'Well, you sure is a sight for sore eyes, Clem,' he called from a distance. 'Still lookin' for gold?'

The old fellow turned his stiff neck to view the lawman. He gave an answering grin to show a mouth almost empty of teeth.

'If it ain't the marshal of Murphy's Ford,' he croaked. 'you missed him by about an hour, I reckon.'

Eli Riley stopped in front of the seated old man. His eyes became suddenly alert.

'Missed who, Clem?' he asked as he squatted down by the little fire with its boiling coffee pot.

'The young fella you's trackin' down, I figure. He was prowlin' round here when I showed up, so I kept under cover. Then he ups and heads northwards. Surely seemed to be one suspicious character, Marshal.'

'What was he doin' here, Clem?'

The old man shrugged and checked the coffee pot.

'Can't rightly say,' he admitted, 'but he was ahead of me about two miles back and checkin' all along the bank of the creek. I didn't reckon him to be prospectin' with a gun at his belt and a carbine

66

in his saddle holster. What's he done?'

'I ain't lookin' for anybody, Clem,' the marshal said as he looked round the scene. 'You tryin' for gold in the creek?'

'Sure am, but I ain't havin' much luck these days. I'm out here because the creeks we was workin' up Lambton way is gettin' all silted up from that damned copper minin' business. I don't reckon to be makin' above three dollars a week lately. Them minin' fellas have been a real kick in the ass to us old panhandlers. You want some coffee?'

The marshal nodded and the old man struggled to his feet. He went across to the mule to unpack another enamel mug. He wiped it clean on the bandanna he wore round his neck and then took down one of the two stone jars that were tied to his saddle bow. He came back to the fire and removed the coffee pot.

'I make a good brew,' he wheezed as he poured the steaming liquid, 'and a little drop of corn mash adds to the taste. Just help yourself.'

The marshal took the mug but waved a hand at the offer of the corn mash.

'You still makin' that stuff yourself, Clem?' he asked.

'Sure am, this is all the original "Oh, be Joyful" with a little raw meat added to help the fermentation. Fellas like me can't afford the prices the townfolk ask for their fancy bottles and labels. This warms the spot, Marshal. I never leave home without a good supply.'

'I'm surprised you've lived so long. That stuff would burn through a cow hide.'

The old prospector chuckled as he sipped the steaming mixture with relish.

'I reckon to be risin' on seventy if my ma was right about my brothers and me. And I reckon as how a daily ration of corn mash has had one hell of a lot to do with it. Now, Marshal, suppose you tell me what you're doin' out this way. It ain't your usual sorta territory.'

'You been to town lately, Clem?'

'No. Ain't had no reason to go there. Got no money and got no dust to be assayed. Why? What's been happenin' in Murphy's Ford?'

Eli told him and watched with some amusement as the old man's face registered surprise and shock. A slightly shaky hand poured more of the corn mash into the tin mug.

'Well, if that don't beat all!' the old prospector wheezed. 'Poor old doc. He was a good man, Marshal. Helped me out when I got that fever last winter. I reckon as how them minin' fellas have a hell of a lot to answer for.'

Eli Riley nodded towards the swiftly flowing creek.

'Do you ever drink this water, Clem?' he asked.

The old man shook his head. 'Never need to,' he said. 'We got a well back where me and the other old panhandlers live. It were dug forty years ago when the first strike made us all a few dollars. Served us proudly it has, with water as sweet as a pretty girl's kiss. I always figured as how the creeks is all poisoned these days anyway. The doc must have reckoned along the same lines. You think he found out too much and them copper-minin' fellas killed him?'

'Could be, but there's a lotta questions that ain't answered yet. I'm trackin' along the creek in the hope of findin' some sign of what Doc Vale was up to. This fella that you saw earlier – what sorta carbine was he carrying?'

'I reckon it would be a Winchester. Why?'

'Curious. Couldn't have been a Spencer?'

'Hell no. He was a young fella. Not some old soldier still hankerin' for a trumpet call to go killin' bluebellies.'

'What was he doin' along the creek, Clem?' the marshal asked patiently.

'Well, he were actin' real peculiar. Walkin' his horse along and peerin' into every clump of cactus and mesquite. He was sure as hell lookin' for some-thin' near the water's edge.'

'Did he find anything?'

'How the hell would I know?' The old man snorted. 'I kept outa sight. He just didn't seem the sorta fella you'd want to argue with. I figured as how he might be from the copper-minin' outfit and was tryin' to find somethin' they'd lost while some diggin' work was bein' done.'

'So he's still ahead of you?'

'He'll be near to the minin' place by now, I reckon. This tale that you've been tellin' me seems to make some sense of what he might have been up to. If the minin' folk is worried about poisonin' the creek, maybe he was lookin' for signs of it.'

The old man stood up and walked a few steps nearer the flowing water. He scooped out a handful of reddish-coloured mud and squeezed the dark ooze out between his fingers.

'This water was runnin' clear last year,' he said. 'All this stuff has drifted down with the flow or been blown by the wind. Them last twisters we had must have dropped a few tons of copper dust around the place. I reckon you can still see the streaks of it all along the ground. Doc Vale could have been right. And that's why he was killed.'

'I'm tryin' to find out what the doc was actually doin' here,' the marshal said grimly. 'He must have had some sorta medicine bag with him, and that ain't turned up. Seen any sign of such a thing, Clem?'

The old man squatted down again and took a sip of his coffee.

'Can't say as I have,' he growled, 'but then I ain't been lookin' for anythin' that don't pan out at sixteen dollars to the ounce. And if you take my advice, Marshal, you won't go no further towards the minin' camp. If they shot the doc, they sure as hell won't be fussy about killin' a lawman. This is as far as I intend to go, and you can lay to that.'

He pointed towards the northern ridges.

'When you reach that crest near them rocks, the folk in the minin' camp can see your dust. That's where the doc might have gone wrong. Somebody could have spotted him and come gallopin' down to do somethin' about it.'

'Yeah, you could be right, Clem, and them folks at the mine will be really on the prod now. They've had trouble back in Murphy's Ford, and some of them have been killed by townsfolk. They got reason to be fightin' mad.'

'Then the best thing you can do is to rest your horse before goin' back to the bright lights. If you get yourself into trouble out here, I ain't gonna play no hero. I'm too old and I'm too scared.'

The two men sat silently drinking for a while until the marshal suddenly had an idea.

'Tell me, Clem,' he said thoughtfully, 'how would a fella like the doc go about testin' the water?'

'Hell, I don't know,' the old prospector growled. 'Them educated fellas got all sorts of ways of doin' tests. Like them assay fellas back in town. I figure as how they use chemicals and such.'

'So he would have to be carryin' a bag, as I supposed?'

'Sure. He wouldn't be drinkin' the water and waitin' to be taken poorly.'

'I reckon as how your mysterious rider might have been lookin' for the same things I'm lookin' for, then. I'd better ride on a mite further. Thanks for the coffee.'

'Now, don't forget. No showin' your head above that far ridge.'

'I'll be careful, Clem. You look after yourself too.'

'I sure as hell aim to do that.'

The marshal got to his feet and went across to tighten the girth on his horse. It had been grazing peacefully next to the mule and puffed out its belly a little to show that it would rather be left in peace. The lawman played his usual trick of tightening the girth and then waiting until the animal relaxed. He gave another quick pull on the buckle and the saddle was safe for the journey.

The sudden noise took both men by surprise for a moment. They looked at each other with blank stares before the sound of the gunshot registered.

Clem jumped to his feet and hurried to the mule where a shotgun was strapped across the pommel of the saddle. He unhooked the weapon and came to stand fearfully at the side of the marshal.

'It was just over that rise,' he whispered as though the gunman was only a few yards away. 'We oughta get the hell outa here.'

Eli Riley unholstered his own Winchester and checked the Colt .44 at his waist.

'You can do what you like, Clem,' he growled, 'but I'm gonna see what's goin' on. That's my job.'

'I ain't ridin' with you.'

'I ain't askin' you to.'

The lawman mounted his horse and swung it towards the slight hill while the old prospector watched and cursed through a toothless mouth. Eli pulled at the reins just before the crown of the ridge was reached. He dismounted and crawled forward across the rough grass until he could see over the gentle slope that went down into a sand-swept layer of soggy ground.

There was nothing in sight for a moment. Just clumps of bushes and tall tufts of wind-blown grass that waved in the breeze. Then he saw a man lying flat on the ground behind a stunted sycamore. He was holding a Winchester and peering round the bole of the tree towards a spot somewhere to the north-east. Eli looked in the same direction and could make out three or four horses that were tethered near a fringe of mesquite. He could see no sign of life around the animals and his attention went back to the man who was aiming the gun.

He seemed to be a youngish fellow, dressed in dark clothes and with a pistol at his waist. His hair was fair and low on his neck. Then the marshal noticed the blood that had soaked through the left sleeve of the short leather jacket that he wore. Eli grimaced and took another look towards the spot at which the wounded man was aiming.

Then he saw them. There were three attackers, crouching low behind bushes and out of sight of the man on the ground. But the lawman could see them from the higher elevation at the top of the ridge. They were gradually crawling round to encircle their victim, and Eli Riley decided to take a hand in the affair.

He raised the Winchester and fired at the one nearest to him. It was a long shot and he could not guarantee hitting the man. His finger squeezed the trigger and the gun barked in satisfying style. A jet of brownish earth shot up just in front of the target. It sent the man scurrying back into the bushes. The wounded man saw the movement and loosed off with his own Winchester. He was nearer and there was a yell of pain that indicated a hit.

The wounded man turned to look up to where Eli Riley was crouching. His face was pale and he raised a damaged left arm in a gesture of thanks. The marshal waved back, even though not quite sure whether or not he was on the right side. Two more shots struck the air as the encircling assailants saw the movements and let fly wildly. One bullet hit a rock near the marshal but it was a wild shot and did not worry him. IIe looked for more movement, but before he could find another target, the whole situation changed.

Two more shots blasted the air in quick succession. They were a lower velocity than Winchester ammunition and it was clear that they came from a shotgun. Old Clem was kneeling near a dead cactus and had blasted away wildly while he cackled with laughter at his own folly. Eli opened fire again. He worked the loading lever furiously as he emptied the carbine. The wounded victim saw what these two strangers were attempting and joined in with a frenzy of firepower.

It worked. The three attackers jumped to their feet and rushed to the tethered horses. One was limping but they were soon mounted and riding off in a haze of dust.

Eli Riley reloaded the Winchester and motioned old Clem to stay where he was. He still did not know the identity of the wounded man and was not going to take any risks. He waited until the young fellow got to his feet, tucked his own Winchester under his damaged arm, and walked slowly up the slope towards the two men who had saved his life.

It was Clem who suddenly broke away from the marshal and hurried towards the stranger with a wide grin on his grizzled face.

'By all that's holy!' he cried as he reached out a hand in greeting. 'I never expected to see young Tom Vale beholden to me and my old shotgun.'

EIGHT

The young man was slimly built and quite tall. His face bore a faint resemblance to Doc Vale but had a deep tan and intensely blue eyes that were now screwed up in pain. He managed to grin at his two rescuers as he came towards them.

'I'm sure glad to see you, Marshal,' he said thankfully, 'and you are certainly a sight for sore eyes, Clem. Pa mentioned you in his last letter. Said as how you was leadin' the prospectors against the mine owners and all the damage they were doin' to the creeks.'

Clem nodded vigorously as he examined the youth's left arm.

'We ain't gettin' enough gold out these days to make a living,' he growled. 'You ain't hurt bad, Tom, but you sure need to get back to town and let the pharmacist fella put some healing stuff on it. Where's your horse?'

'The first shot sent it gallopin' off down the hill

some place. It'll end up at the creek, like as not. I'll go look.'

Clem held him back. 'I'll go,' the old man volunteered. 'You tie your bandanna round that while you're tellin' this worried lawman what the hell you was doin' out here. We both had you figured for one of the minin' fellas.'

The old prospector started towards the creek and then suddenly stopped to turn and confront the marshal.

'I figure as I did a real fool thing back there,' he said thoughtfully. 'An old fella like me firin' off at professional gunslingers. Ain't as if I was even deputized. I reckon you would have pinned a star on me if there'd been time, so maybe I got some posse money comin' anyways.'

He looked quizzically at the marshal and broke into a broad grin when the lawman nodded.

'I figure you for a day's pay, Clem,' Eli Riley said with judicial gravity. 'Just call into the office next time you're in town and I'll fix it up.'

The old prospector went off cheerfully to capture the missing horse while the other two men concentrated on bandaging the arm wound. It was merely a shallow gash that bled profusely and the young man cut up his bandanna to use as padding and a tourniquet. Eli Riley folded his own bandanna to hold the pad in place. He knotted the stained cloth and nodded his satisfaction at a job well done.

'I'm sorry about your ma and pa,' he said as he wiped his bloodied hands on the grass. 'I take it that the preacher sent you word by telegraph.'

'Yes. I was only a day's ride from Murphy's Ford. I had a job at a saloon in Fort Rice. Just keepin' the peace there, is all. I got to your town last night, and the preacher told me the whole story. I was pretty shaken. My pa was no troublemaker but he'd been worried over that water for a few weeks. He wrote me about it, and I knew he was plannin' to test the supply from the creek.'

'So what was you doin' out here?'

'I stayed with Preacher Edwards and his wife last night. Gave me a chance to think things over. Then I decided to see what happened to the tests Pa was makin' at the creek. He had to have some ways of measurin' the amount of stuff in the water. So I came out here and started back-trackin' him.'

Eli nodded. 'That's what I was doin' when I ran into Clem. I shoulda done it earlier but so much has been happenin' in town that this was the first chance I got. Did you find anything?'

The young man nodded eagerly. 'Yes, and that's why them fellas got me off guard. There's a clump of mesquite down by the creek. Somethin' was reflectin' the sunlight and I got down to take a look. It was a broken test tube. Just the sorta thing my pa would be usin' if he was checkin' the water with any sort of chemicals. I found some deep ruts from a four-wheeled rig and a few horse droppings

78

as well. I'd just started to push through the mesquite when them three fellas jumped me. You came along just in time.'

'Yeah. Me and Clem has taken over from the Seventh Cavalry. Do you feel up to finishin' what you started, fella?'

The young man nodded eagerly.

'Yeah. Let's go take another look,' he suggested cheerfully. 'I'd just spotted somethin' else when they started shootin' and I had to dive for cover.'

The two men walked a little way down the slope until they reached an untidy row of bushes that overhung part of the creek. Clem joined them with his mule and the two horses in tow. He watched as Tom knelt down and pointed out the broken glass to the lawman. Eli Riley started searching among the dusty branches and suddenly pulled out a leather Gladstone bag that was greened with mildew and had a few insects crawling over it. The bag was opened and contained a few more pieces of broken glass.

Clem joined the search and found a small book with pages eaten away. It was a scientific publication such as Doc Morton had mentioned.

'Your pa was surely here,' the marshal said sadly. He looked at a little coil of soft iron wire and raised a quizzical eyebrow.

'What the hell's that for?' he asked.

Clem grinned and took it off him.

'Just watch,' he said. He unrolled a few inches of

the metal and went down to the edge of the water. He dipped the piece of wire into the swiftly moving flow and knelt patiently for a few minutes. Young Tom watched intently despite his injured arm. The marshal used the time to reload his Winchester and place it back in the saddle holster. There was a sudden shout of triumph as the old prospector waved the wire in the air.

It now bore a rusty tinge that showed up clearly in the bright sunlight.

'The creek's poisoned!' Clem shouted as he handed the coil to the marshal. 'Iron turns red in copper-poisoned water. And that's good enough proof for any crooked lawyer.'

'He's right,' Tom Vale said grimly. 'I remember readin' somethin' like that back East. The folks in Murphy's Ford have got a right to be sore if they're drinkin' this stuff. Them copper fellas killed my pa because he could prove them guilty.'

Eli Riley looked sourly at the wire before handing it back to Clem.

'Could be rust,' he said dismissively. 'Now, let's not be in too much of a rush about this. I've been doin' a lotta thinkin' on what's been happenin' around here, and I ain't sure yet. Let's just go into town and have a word with the mayor.'

'There'll be one hell of a barnstormin' when the folks in Murphy's Ford hear about Tom bein' shot by the minin' fellas,' Clem said with relish. 'I figure as how the town will go killin' mad.'

'That's what I'm afraid of,' the marshal said. 'And they might go killin' the wrong people all over again.'

He turned to the young man who was nursing his injured arm.

'You've built yourself quite a reputation as a gunslinger,' he said. 'But I don't like folk usin' guns around my town. I'd hate to think that you'd be talkin' people into makin' trouble before we really know what's been happenin' to the water supply.'

'I would have thought we already know,' Tom Vale answered quietly. There was an edge to his voice and the lawman could see the change in the sudden coldness of his face.

'You and I should be on the same side in this,' the marshal said, 'and I don't aim to have anythin' unlawful happenin' in my neck of the woods. Do we understand each other?'

'You already have somethin' unlawful happenin' around here,' the young man said flatly. 'And I aim to get even for the deaths of my ma and pa. I don't figure to let anybody stand in the way of that. It's what I call justice, and the law don't come within spittin' distance of it.'

'You're talkin' about revenge, son.'

Tom Vale nodded. 'That's the best type of justice.'

'Only if you get the real villains.'

'I'll get them.'

The words were quietly spoken but sounded as deadly as any gunshot.

NINE

It was not a quiet night in Murphy's Ford. Both saloons were crowded and noisy as people discussed all that had happened. Their voices were angry and got louder as more bad whiskey went down their throats. Marshal Riley had his deputies patrolling the streets in the early part of the evening. But they vanished before midnight and he guessed that he would not be able to find them if trouble started.

Old Clem was the cause of it all. He had gone back to town in good spirits at the thought of picking up his posse money. After a visit to the jailhouse and the pharmacist with young Tom Vale he headed for the Palomino saloon. Already fired by his own corn mash, he was soon talking of what happened by the creek, His own heroism was not overlooked and the number of attackers grew in the telling. Ten or twelve were driven off with plenty of dead or wounded. The marshal had been a help, but old Clem and his trusty shotgun had really won the day.

He told them about the iron wire changing colour in the polluted water, and mentioned the traces found of Doc Vale's rig and the broken glass. One man in particular took in every word the drunken prospector uttered. Peter Murphy had a good store that supported his wife and two young children. Both of his daughters were still sick and Doc Vale had been treating them. It was their problems, and those of other ailing youngsters, that had made the doctor suspicious of the creek water.

'We gotta do somethin' about this,' the store owner told his drinking companions. 'The mayor ain't gonna move and the marshal won't budge off his ass unless the councilmen order him to go out there with a posse and close that minin' business down before we all get poisoned.'

'So what do we do?' one of the other men asked.

There was a slight silence while Peter Murphy tried to put his thoughts in some sort of order.

'We could form our own posse,' he said slowly. 'Ride out there and shoot the place up. Most of them workers is foreign fellas. They ain't got guns and they'd run like hell as soon as they saw us comin' over the hill. We already got their gunslinger so I reckon they'd all quit the place to save their hides.'

There was a general nodding of heads and the few who did not agree were too scared to voice an opinion.

Clem gave a loud cough to draw attention to himself.

'There's a fella in town who's one hell of a gunslinger,' he said slyly. 'He's a bit shot-up hisself at the moment, but he knows what it's all about. And he'd sure be willin' to help us out.'

'You're talkin' about Doc Vale's son?' Peter Murphy asked.

'Sure am. He's goin' all out to avenge the murder of his folks. And he ain't scared of the marshal or them damn-fool deputies of his either. I reckon he'd shoot them as soon as look at them.'

'He's stayin' with the preacher, ain't he?' Peter Murphy asked thoughtfully. Clem nodded and the store owner continued.

'Suppose I call on him,' he suggested, 'and tell him that he'll have the support of every decent man in town. Then we can ride out there and finish them troublemakers for good and all.'

He looked round the saloon.

'Are you with me?'

There was an almost unanimous shout of agreement.

The other saloon was also discussing the problem, but in a more dignified manner. It was a place that people like the mayor and the bank manager frequented. They sat at polished wooden tables and drank good whiskey out of clean glasses. They were there now, after a long and earnest council meeting.

Mayor Hadley would have preferred the privacy of his own hotel, but the councilmen had headed straight for the Golden Globe. He had joined them to make sure that any further discussions went the right way.

The meeting of the town council had gone well. Nobody there had wanted the copper mining company to be harmed in any way. They all agreed that the town was in need of industry and what it could bring. Small store owners like Peter Murphy did not count with the big earners of Murphy's Ford. Clean linen and curtains were not in demand by copper miners. It was people like the mayor who supplied the company as did the big hardware and food stores. And above them all towered the banker who reigned over a prosperous business that owed its success directly and indirectly to the copper industry.

'Why doesn't the marshal run this Tom Vale out of town?' Leo Ramsay had asked as he stroked his massive sideburns with loving fingers.

'I did suggest that,' the mayor said sadly, 'but Eli Riley told me that the fella ain't done nothin' wrong. And we have to remember that he's Doc Vale's son. He's gotta deal with his pa's property before he leaves town. And what would folk say if we sent him on his way before he could settle things and pay his respects at the grave?'

There was a mournful nodding of heads.

The judge shifted in his chair and the other

councilmen paid him the attention he expected.

'I reckon as how you're all worryin' over noth-ing,' old Vic Lester said in his crackling voice. 'The kids will get better in the next few days. That'll set minds at rest. Then old Clem will drink up what money he has and leave town again. Young Tom Vale ain't got no friends here in Murphy's Ford. Folk don't know him, and his reputation as a failed lawman and a hired gun ain't gonna help. Just sit your horses firmly and it'll pass away. We just gotta make our peace with the copper boss and ignore all this dime novel stuff about wire turnin' all the colours of a magic lantern.'

'I hope you're right,' the mayor said devoutly.

It was at that point that the meeting broke up.

One of the few men not drinking that night was Marshal Riley. He sat in his office with a pack of solitaire cards in front of him. They were ignored as he edgily waited for trouble to start some-where in town. His only consolation was that none of the copperminers was visiting. He knew who the troublemakers would be, and he also knew that if violence broke out he would be on his own.

The lawman began to doze after a while. It was just after one in the morning when he stirred in his heavy chair. He glanced at the Viennese wall clock as he got slowly to his feet and crossed to the window. He looked out on the main street. Things seemed quiet enough and he began to hope that his fears had been groundless. He strapped on his gun and decided to take a walk through town. It was the Palomino saloon that was the hot spot for any potential trouble, but to his surprise, the place was quiet and half-empty.

He scratched his head and stared at the brightly lit saloon as he listened to the few voices that floated out to the quiet street. He crossed to the swing doors and looked over them at the drinkers inside the building. There was no sign of old Clem or Tom Vale. It seemed like any other night and the marshal shook his head in bewilderment and walked slowly away.

He glanced in at the Golden Globe just as a precaution. It was getting ready to close and only the judge sat at his usual table waiting for one of his sons to collect him. Eli Riley returned to the jailhouse a puzzled but relieved man. He decided to go home for the rest of the night. It would disturb his wife, but a rousting from her was a small price to pay for a peaceful town.

He had put out two of the oil lamps when a quiet tapping at the back door drew his attention. He went down the short passageway and stood with one hand on the butt of the Colt at his side.

'Who's there?' he demanded.

The voice that answered was hard to understand until the marshal shouted again.

'Ezra Davis.' The voice was a little louder and Eli

opened the door to let the scared little man into the jailhouse.

'What the hell are you doin' here at this time of night, Ezra?' he demanded as he led the way to his office.

His visitor was a wispy figure in a neat black coat and freshly laundered shirt. His grey moustache and untidy hair framed a pale, bony face. He wore narrow, gold-rimmed glasses that magnified his damp eyes. Ezra ran the pharmacy and had a thriving business. Folks went to him when they could not afford a doctor. He and his stringy wife lived above the store but did not seem to be part of the town élite.

'You look as if you could use a drink.' the marshal said sympathetically as he pulled forward a bentwood chair. The man nodded eagerly and swallowed what he was given in two hasty gulps. Eli waited until the glass was placed down on the desk and promptly refilled it for him.

'You seem to have troubles,' he said as he sipped his own small drink.

'I ain't got them, Eli, but this town surely has,' the man said in a nervous voice. 'This is just between you and me, remember. I can't be seen talkin' to the law, nohow. I gotta live among these folks.'

Eli sat down. 'So tell me,' he prompted.

Ezra gulped noisily and then began his story. He told about all the talk in the Palomino saloon and the decision to raid the copper-mining camp. His good memory enabled him to quote practically every word that had passed. The marshal listened with mounting alarm.

'And you don't go along with it, Ezra? You ain't mad at the copper fellas?' the lawman asked when the tale was told.

The misty eyes narrowed a little as the little man smiled reluctantly.

'I got a funny sort of position in this town, Eli,' he said sadly. 'As a pharmacist, I don't get respect from the doctors or their friends. Doc Vale and Doc Morton made up their own medicines, and I'm left with the tail-end of the business. They don't even bother with my wife and me in a social sort of way. Hurts her bad, that does. That's why I do my drinkin' in the Palomino. I got some respect among ordinary folks.'

Eli nodded his understanding. 'I guess so,' he said slowly, 'but I would have thought that'd put you against the miners.'

The man shook his head vigorously. 'It ain't that simple,' he said. 'The minin' company order medical supplies from me. They don't have to but it's a sorta gesture of goodwill on their part. I'd be hit as badly as any of the fellas on the town council if the mine closed. You gotta stop that raid, Eli.'

'Yeah. I can see me doin' it without any deputies, and all the guns in the town against me. Is Tom Vale goin' to lead this lynchin' party?'

'No, he's outa action for a week or so. They're settin' out in the mornin' but his arm is still bad. Infection's set in and I don't reckon he'll be ridin' anywhere until the medication starts to work. What are you goin' to do, Eli?'

'I'll go see the mayor and spoil his sleep. He's the boss around here and the only one who can order out a posse. There won't be enough fellas in town to make one up, and I don't imagine the councilmen rushin' to volunteer. My guess is that the raid will go through and there'll be one hell of a fight. Some of the minin' folk must have guns, and even if the labourers run for it, there'll still be some shootings.'

'I reckon so. Just don't mention my name.'

The mayor took the news badly. He sat at his desk after Eli Riley had left and tapped nervously on the woodwork with trembling fingers. His son sat opposite him. His attitude was much calmer and his cold eyes watched his father with a certain contempt. Both men were in their nightclothes and quilted dressing-gowns.

'We can't let this happen,' the mayor groaned. 'Eli Riley's no use and those two damned deputies seem to have left town. What the hell can we do, Jim?'

His son was already thinking out the situation and spoke without hesitation.

'I can ride out and get to the mine before the

folks in town think of settin' off. If the company has warnin' enough, they can set a trap in Gormley's Gorge. It's a narrow trail there with plenty of cover. That mob might never even reach the mine.'

The mayor brightened slightly and rose from his chair. He picked up the glass-chambered oil lamp and carried it over to the coloured map on the wall.

'That's the answer,' he said in a relieved voice. 'You go and get yourself dressed while I saddle your horse.'

He put the lamp back on the desk, and as his son was leaving the room, Bert Hadley called him back.

'You and me has had a few fallings-out lately, Jim,' he said warmly, 'but we're family, son. Don't get yourself mixed up in what happens and come back safe.'

There were nearly forty horsemen gathered outside the Palomino saloon just after dawn. Most were armed with revolvers and some had shotguns or carbines. Old Clem was not among them. He had drunk his fill and let the mule guide him back to his timber shack a short way out of town.

Tom Vale came to see them off. His arm was in a sling and his face was pale after a restless night. He talked with the leaders and waved as the horses galloped out of town in a wall of dust. They were headed north and he stood watching until they were out of sight.

Somebody else was watching. The mayor stood behind the curtained windows of the hotel and noted every face in the crowd. He had a pencil in his hand and wrote down the names on a large sheet of paper which he rested on an account book. Those names would be useful at a later date.

People who owed money to the bank or who wanted favours from the councilmen might find themselves in difficulties. The mayor was beginning to relish the situation and was eager to get a report from his son.

Murphy's Ford was an empty town. With most of the stores closed and so many horses missing the place was as still as a go-to-meeting Sunday. Marshal Riley sat in his office. The bank manager and the mayor drank whiskey on the hotel stoop while the mortician got ready for some extra business.

Nothing happened.

Dusk was falling when Jim Hadley rode back into town. He tethered his animal to the rail outside the hotel and wearily mounted the steps. His father and the moneylender had long since given up their watch and only a couple of guests sat smoking cigars. They nodded to the manager but received the barest acknowledgement as he passed through the door to stalk across the foyer towards the private quarters in the rear.

Mayor Hadley was having his dinner and his wife was sitting with him. He jumped up excitedly at the appearance of his son.

'Well, lad,' he gasped eagerly as he threw down his napkin, 'What happened at Gormley's Gorge?'

The young man did not answer right away. He picked up the glass water jug and took a long swig. Then he breathed a sigh of content and looked at his father for the first time.

'Nothin' happened at the gorge,' he said angrily. 'They never turned up.'

'That can't be,' the mayor protested. 'A whole crowd of them left here early this morning. I watched them go. Damn it, lad, they had to turn up. I'm tellin' you. I watched them ride outa town.'

Jim Hadley sat down wearily. 'Pa, I got to the mine and warned Ross Kimber. He saw the sense of makin' a stand at the gorge. I waited while he lined up every gun he had. There were even sticks of blastin' powder ready to blow them raiders apart. I rode out with the minin' fellas and we waited all day. They just didn't arrive. That mine is as safe as it ever was.'

The mayor stood silently for a moment. Then he sat down heavily and rested his elbows on the white cloth.

'I don't figure it,' he said softly. 'We've lost half the town somehow or other. Where the hell can they be?'

Tom Vale planned it well. He and Clem had discussed the poisoning of the water at great length. The young man's arm was aching and the pharmacist had warned him that the infection might take weeks to clear. With Clem's local knowledge, a good way of hitting at the mining company had been worked out that was far more effective and a lot less dangerous than a Seventh Cavalry charge by a mob of amateurs.

Peter Murphy listened to what the two men had to say and began to see the sense of their planning. When the riders left town early the next morning, their destination was not the mining camp. They headed north under the watchful eye of the mayor, but once out of town, they gradually moved west and rode across a flat and open plain with few trees and little grass. The cactus plants stood high in the arid ground and the heat of the sun began to tell on the riders.

They eventually stopped at a small creek that bubbled down from some low hills. Water bottles were refilled and the horses refreshed. The men rested for a while and then remounted to finish their journey in the late afternoon.

The sun was low on the horizon when they reached their goal. The telegraph poles were the first things to be seen in the distance. They ran parallel with the railroad line and made a good perch for hungry birds to scan their prey.

The shining steel rails ran straight and true on a slight embankment. They were new and had been partly financed by the mining company. They branched from the main west to east line some thirty miles away and ended at the mine amid the rich loads of copper ore that were ready for ship-ment.

The railroad was a welcome sight and there were whoops of triumph as the men dismounted and began their task. By the time they were finished, the mines would be isolated and the long-awaited steam shovels would be stranded up north.

TEN

Mayor Hadley held the meeting in his office at the feed store while his son rested after his adventures. It was more private than the hotel and the few guests staying there had been disturbed by recent events in Murphy's Ford. There were just four people round the desk. The mayor took pride of place with the judge opposite him. They occupied the two comfortable upholstered chairs. Marshal Riley and Leo Ramsay had to be content with the bentwood chairs that creaked at every movement. There was no whiskey. It was too early in the day.

'Even two of my own men left town with that wild mob,' Bert Hadley moaned. 'I'll give them their time if they ever turn up again. If any harm's been done to the minin' company, this town is finished. We'll never get the railroad extended and we'll all be ruined.'

'Well, they didn't raid the mine,' the judge pointed out quietly. 'We've at least that much to be thankful for.'

'So where the hell are they?' Leo Ramsay asked sharply.

They all looked at the marshal and he blinked rapidly as he realized that he was expected to supply an answer.

'I could question old Clem,' he said quietly, 'or have a word with Tom Vale if he's up to it. I'd have done it sooner but we was all expectin' them fellas to be back in town long before now.'

The mayor nodded agreement. 'Go see Clem,' he advised. 'He'll talk if you wave drinkin' money under his nose. That young Vale fella might be more difficult. If Clem won't talk, drag him into town and sling the old fool into the jailhouse. A few days without a drop of corn mash will soon change his mind.'

'You can't do that,' said the judge.

He had spent most of the meeting eyeing the whiskey bottle on the shelf behind the desk.

'And why can't we do it?' the mayor demanded to know. 'Do we run this town or do we leave it in the hands of a lynch mob?'

'Old Clem ain't done nothin' you can arrest him for,' the judge pointed out. 'You can ask questions, and you can even tell him he ain't welcome in Murphy's Ford no more. But if you go lockin' him up, you gotta charge him with somethin' and give him his day in court. That's the law. At least I think it is.'

'Well, I reckon you know the law,' the banker

chuckled. 'you've certainly abused it often enough.'

The mayor banged his fist on the desk. 'Are you tellin' me that I can't even run my own town? These fellas are out raidin' somewhere or other. I've got the names of most of them and I don't aim they should ruin Murphy's Ford and get away with it. And old Clem knows all about their activities.'

'Well, we don't rightly know what they're doin' out there in the wilds at the present time,' the judge muttered as he sadly took his eyes off the distant bottle. 'Maybe they all just went to a psalm-singin' gatherin' down by the river. Is the preacher still in town?'

'This is not funny,' the mayor snapped.

'No, it ain't,' the judge agreed. 'But you gotta show that these folk caused trouble, Bert. Then you gotta think about tryin' to arrest just about every gun-totin' fella in town. I don't think Eli Riley could find room in the jailhouse for them all. And he sure won't have any deputies helpin' him round them up. If I was in the marshal's boots, I'd be lookin' for a quieter job right now.'

'The judge has a point,' Leo Ramsay said thoughtfully. 'The folk that have ridden out are the backbone of this town. We can't go making enemies of them all. No matter what happens.'

He turned to the marshal.

'Look, Eli, why not have a word with Clem as the mayor suggests. Press a dollar or two into his palm if you have to, but treat him gentle-like. We have to put right any trouble these folks cause. We need the mine, and if they only thought about it, so do they. This town has a future, but it has to endure a few problems on the way. If the creek is poisoned, then maybe we can arrange some remedy. We could even dig more wells or divert water from that small creek up Wyford way. There are methods of getting out of all this trouble if we just use our heads.'

The mayor nodded eagerly. 'I like what you're saying, Leo,' he said as he reached up for the whiskey bottle. It was a sign that the outlook was improving. It certainly was for the judge. His eyes glowed as he took the offered glass and raised it to his lips. Before he could take the first sip, a loud knock on the door made all four men sit up nervously. They looked at each other with a certain foreboding.

The caller was the telegraph operator. He was still in his shirtsleeves and panting slightly after the hurried trip from his office at the other end of town.

'I got bad news, Mr Mayor,' he gasped ominously. 'The lines are down.'

'From both directions?' It was the marshal who asked.

'Only from the Tombstone end. The eastern line is still workin' but the folk at that end don't know any more than I do. We're cut off from the

100

north and the west.'

The men at the desk looked at each other silently for a moment.

'That line runs along the railroad,' Leo Ramsay said slowly. 'I reckon as how we know what's happened now.'

The mayor nodded dumbly and swallowed his whiskey as if in an act of desperation.

'They've attacked the railroad and pulled down the telegraph line,' he moaned softly. 'We're in real trouble. It won't be a local matter any more. There'll be federal marshals on our necks and all sorts of official inquiries. They might even send in some troops.'

The mayor turned to the marshal.

'Eli, you gotta make Clem tell us what was planned.'

The marshal nodded and rose to leave the office. Clem's small hut was at least a mile away. It was one of several in a little group near old gold-mine workings that had petered out years ago. Eli was in half a mind to saddle his horse but decided that he perhaps needed a little exercise. The journey was wasted. The prospector and his mule were missing.

Another old-timer was chopping wood outside his own shanty. He told the marshal that Clem and the others were trying their luck at Kinnock Creek and had left early that morning. The creek was a two-day journey there and back, so Eli was out of luck. He shrugged his shoulders and headed back for Murphy's Ford.

It was still a deathly quiet place and he retired to his jailhouse. Another meeting with the mayor was not something he welcomed and he decided that a cup of coffee and some bacon would be a good way of passing the time. Eli Riley felt completely at a loss. There did not seem to be anything he could do that would help the situation. He really felt despondent enough to quit the job. Only the fact that it would make his wife a happy woman made him hesitate.

The sound of horses interrupted his thoughts and he crossed to the window to watch the return of the raiders. But he was wrong. The town folk were not making a victorious entry after their vigilante activities. It was a group of about twelve horsemen around a large four-wheeled carriage which was drawn by two well-groomed animals. He recognized the man who sat comfortably on the leather seating. The head of the copper company had come to town.

Ross Kimber's carriage drew up outside the Hadley House hotel, and while the riders grouped protectively around their boss, the driver of the rig got down and opened the door of the vehicle. The mine boss alighted, his heavy bulk tilting the rig as he lumbered on to the stoop and looked around him.

The mine boss was an impressive-looking man.

His clothes were well-tailored in pale grey and his dark eyes were alert under heavy brows. He had a large moustache and held a cigar in his gloved right hand. The door of the hotel swung open and young Jim Hadley came out to greet the visitor. He stopped to stare at the large escort but gathered his wits quickly enough to hold the door open and beckon Ross Kimber to enter.

'Your pa at home?' The words were curt and unfriendly and young Jim Hadley blinked under the gaze of the man he faced.

'He's at the grain store,' he said. 'It's just at the end of the main street. Round the corner by the corrals.'

'I know where it is and I ain't goin' chasin' small-town mayors. Go tell your pa to get himself here *muy pronto*.'

Jim Hadley's narrow face flushed with anger and he opened his mouth to say something. Then he changed his mind and turned on his heel to re-enter the hotel. The clerk at the large mahogany counter looked up as his boss stormed across the foyer.

'Go down to the grain store and tell my father that Mr Kimber wants to see him,' he ordered.

The clerk hurried round the counter and left the building without making any comment. He had heard the brief conversation on the stoop and had no wish to argue. Ross Kimber followed Jim Hadley into the hotel. He took a seat at one of the small tables, nodded pleasantly enough to the two guests who were drinking coffee nearby, and waited with his arms folded.

Jim Hadley hesitated for a moment and then went back to the office. His thin face was set in passionate lines of anger.

The mayor came hurrying in a few minutes later. The clerk followed and went back to his position behind the counter. Bert Hadley greeted the visitor with an unctuous smile and held out a hand that was ignored. Ross Kimber got to his feet.

'Let's go somewhere private,' he said sharply.

Bert Hadley led the way to the office where his son was already pouring out the best whiskey and then making himself inconspicuous by the window.

'And what can I do for you, Mr Kimber?' the mayor asked as he offered the well-filled glass.

'I got a few things to tell you and that council that need sayin' bluntly,' the mine boss said as he took the drink. 'Someone from this town was up by the creek yesterday and my men caught him tryin' to poison the water. There was a shoot-out and some fellas interfered to save the man from bein' caught. One of them was wearin' a marshal's badge. They tell me his name is Riley.'

'Well, didn't Jim tell you what happened?' the mayor pleaded. 'It was young Tom Vale tryin' to trace back where his father had been investigatin' along the creek. The marshal came to his help when he found him bein' attacked. It was all a mistake.'

Ross Kimber shook his head.

'I don't think so,' he snapped. 'I've spent a mint of money on havin' that creek checked for poisonin' of any sort. The water is as clear as it ever was . . .' he paused for effect '. . . until you reach the point where that fella was caught. That's where the poisonin' starts. Somebody is fillin' the creek with copper salts of some sort. A few gallons of sulphate at regular intervals that gets carried on to Murphy's Ford. You gotta look closer to home for your poisoner, and stop blamin' us.'

The mayor was sweating and he swallowed his drink at a single gulp.

'But this town needs the mine,' he whined. 'Why should anyone from here poison the creek?'

'That's for you to find out. Get that marshal off his ass and start him earnin' a living. And I don't like that scare about a lynch mob of vigilantes headin' for the mine. We'd have shot the hell out of them all if they'd turned up. And in case they start talkin' big the next time they're drunk, you can tell them that. I'm glad to see they had a change of heart.'

The mayor poured himself another drink. His hand trembled as he did so.

'Well, there is another problem, Mr Kimber,' he said in a meek voice. 'That mob did set out from here, but they didn't go to the mine. We think they

105

headed for the railroad instead.'

'The railroad!' Ross Kimber had trouble getting the words out. 'The railroad! Are you certain?'

Bert Hadley nodded miserably. 'We're pretty certain. The telegraph wires are down and they haven't got back to town yet. I can't think of any other explanation.'

The mine boss put down the glass of whiskey that he had not touched. He strode to the door and turned as he threw it open.

'I have two steam shovels comin' to the mine in the next week,' he said tautly. 'If they don't arrive on time, I'm goin' to have to advise the directors of the company that work in this area is not worth the effort. There are other mines, and other towns. We want to live at peace with the local folks, but this sort of thing can't go on. You can tell that council of yours just what's goin' to happen. Good day to you.'

Ross Kimber left the office while the mayor and his son stood looking at each other in speechless horror. They missed the arrival of Tom Vale. He was standing in the middle of the foyer when the mine boss made his appearance. The young man still had his left arm in a sling and his face was pale and sweating. He had seen the riders enter town, and his host, the preacher, had identified the man in the carriage. Despite the protests of the Reverend Edwards, Tom Vale had strapped on his gun and set out for the Hadley House hotel.

106

Ross Kimber stopped in the middle of his stride at the confrontation. He eyed the young man uneasily.

'If it's the manager you want,' he said in an attempt at a normal tone, 'he's in the office back there.'

'It's you I want.' Tom Vale's voice was hard and menacing. 'Your men killed my pa because he found out that the creek was poisoned. Then they came into town and battered my ma to death. Well, it's just you and me now, fella.'

Ross Kimber threw open his coat.

'I'm not armed,' he said quietly, 'and them horsemen out there are not goin' to let you survive a shoot-out. I'm sorry about your folks, son. Real sorry. But I've just been tellin' your mayor that the creek was poisoned by somebody from this town. I don't know their reasons, but they got some grudge against us. You go talk with Hadley. He can tell you what we discussed.'

'I don't go along with that. And I don't go along with you not bein' armed either. My pa wrote me that you carry a derringer in your back pants pocket. And that's just where you're reachin' now.'

Ross Kimber's right hand was already behind his back and both men drew almost at the same moment. A single shot echoed round the foyer and a shower of glass fell like a curtain between the two opponents. Their guns had not been fired and both men stood like statues as they stared at the cascade of crystal that spread on the carpet between them.

'Don't let's get any more ideas about shootin' up my town.'

The voice was that of Eli Riley. He stood in the doorway with a shotgun in his hands and looked ready to use it again. He had come along from the jailhouse and stared down the men outside the hotel. Then he waited until Tom Vale and Ross Kimber were ready to kill each other. Shattering the expensive chandelier had been almost a pleasure and he watched the pieces fall to the floor with a grin on his face.

'I suggest you leave town while you still can, Mr Kimber,' he said in his official voice. 'You've got a dozen men out there who are not professional gunfighters and my deputies have got them well and truly nailed down. The vigilantes will also be back here any time now. What do you think they're likely to do to you and that collection of varmint chasers?'

Ross Kimber put the derringer away and tried to look as dignified as possible.

'I've made my position clear, Marshal,' he said. 'This young fella has got it all wrong, but I can understand his feelings.'

He turned to where Mayor Hadley stood by the recettion desk.

'You know the position, Mr Mayor,' he said coldly. 'This will be a federal matter if that railroad is disrupted. Good day to you all.'

He left the hotel and they could hear him getting into the carriage. The sound of the departing horses was loud in the silence of the building. Eli Riley took the pistol off Tom Vale and grasped the young man's right arm.

'I've got a nice cosy cell for you, young fella,' he said. 'You can lodge there until the mayor and the council decide whether or not they want you in town.'

'I think you ought to leave, Tom,' Bert Hadley said in a persuasive voice. 'You're a focus for trouble here. Just wind up your pa's affairs and then be on your way.'

The young man did not answer. He left the building at the side of the marshal. The two walked along the street in silence and Tom was soon seated on a bunk in the jailhouse. He found to his surprise that the lawman had not bothered to lock the cell door. He accepted the cup of coffee gratefully and sat sipping it while the marshal leaned against the open doorway.

'Now, let me tell you something, young fella,' Eli Riley said quietly. 'Your pa was killed by someone who stole bullets from a local store. That same person could ride back into town without anybody noticing. Your ma opened the door and let that person into the house. He wasn't some stranger from outside Murphy's Ford.'

Tom Vale stood up. 'Why should a local fella

want to kill my folks, Marshal?' he asked. 'It don't make sense.'

'Yes, it does. If your pa had just been out on the range and ended up dead, nobody would have thought of blamin' the copper folk. It would have been put down to a hold-up of sorts. But it went wrong because old Doc Morton knew why your pa was out at the creek. Once word got around that he was checkin' for poison, all the blame fell on the minin' company. The killer didn't know that Doc Vale had been speakin' to the only other medico in town. That's where we all got to lookin' at things back to front.'

Tom Vale took another sip of coffee and then sat down again. He hugged the mug between his hands.

'Then who was poisonin' the creek?' he asked.

'I think I know the answer to that one,' the marshal said slowly. 'I hope I'm wrong, but I fancy I know who, and I fancy I know why.'

ELEVEN

The Hadley House hotel was now the centre of attention. A crowd had gathered outside it, peering in at the windows and discussing what had happened. The mayor and his son were trying to pacify the few guests while the broken glass was cleared away. When things quietened down a little, Bert Hadley decided to go to the jailhouse and have a word with the marshal.

He found Eli Riley in the corral at the rear of the building. The lawman was harnessing his horse and had placed saddlebags across its back. He also appeared well-armed and a Winchester was in the long saddle holster ready for use.

'Where the hell are you off to, Eli?' the mayor demanded angrily. 'We need you in town right now. That mob is due back any minute and the devil alone knows what sort of mood they'll be in. Headin' for the saloon to celebrate, like as not.'

'I'm goin' to arrest the fella what poisoned the creek,' the marshal said calmly.

'And who the hell is that?'

'If I'm right, it's old Clem. If not him, then one of the other prospectors. Maybe all of them.'

The mayor thought about it for a moment.

'But how in tarnation can you know that?' he asked. 'Old Clem and the others had no call to go makin' trouble for the town.'

The marshal tightened the girth on his animal and then turned to face the mayor.

'I could be wrong,' he said slowly, 'but them prospectors have suffered badly through the activities of the minin' company. Clem admitted as much to me. If they could make us turn against the copper fellas and get them to close down the workings, it would sure help clear some of the creeks and stop the rest bein' filled up with rubble and stuff. Them new steam shovels would make matters worse. You gotta see their side of things, Mayor.'

'I don't give a damn about their side of things,' Bert Hadley stormed. 'We've gotta think of the town. How sure are you about this?'

'When I saw Clem up at the creek he had his usual corn mash with him. But there were two stone jars of it across the back of the mule. I didn't think about it at the time, but even Clem wouldn't take two jars of the stuff with him. I reckon one of them had the copper poison in it.'

112

'Then you believe he killed Doc Vale?'

'No, but Clem sure set up the situation for it to happen.'

The mayor stood silently for a few moments. He scratched the side of his face and stared about restlessly.

'It's all too late,' he muttered sadly. 'When that damned mob comes back to town they're gonna be boastin' about how they've uprooted the railroad, pulled down the telegraph lines, and generally made things hell for the mine owners. Then I'll have to confirm the bad news to Ross Kimber, and that'll be the end of Murphy's Ford. We'll all be ruined.'

He turned sadly away before recalling something else.

'Them deputies you were tellin' Ross Kimber you had outside the hotel,' he mused with a slight smile, 'where the hell did you get them?'

'I invented them. And they don't even have to be paid. Those fellas ridin' with Kimber were quite upset when I told them that there were four shotguns coverin' them if they as much as scratched their butts. Tamed 'em real well, it did.'

'It's the only good news I've had all day,' the mayor said quietly. 'And what about young Tom Vale? He might have killed Kimber back there. And you've certainly ruined a damned good chandelier. Straight from Chicago, that came. Cost one helluva lotta money, it did.'

113

'A funeral would have cost more.' The marshal grinned. 'I'm holdin' young Tom for the time being. You wanted him outa town and this is as good an excuse as any. He can arrange his pa's affairs, and then we can turn him loose with orders not to come back again. If I'm right about Clem, then Tom Vale will have made a fool of himself and won't be like to cause no more trouble.'

The mayor nodded. 'I hope you're right, Eli. Don't be gone too long.'

'You've still got the two deputies you gave me,' the marshal told him drily, 'if you can find them.'

The old cabin that Clem used was a short journey by horse and stood with five others that were as worn and near to falling down as his. There were a couple of corrals and a small well with three or four wooden pails stored nearby. A solitary mule occupied the corral nearest the huts and chewed on the grass as it ignored the world around it. Smoke came from the iron stovepipe of one of the cabins and an old fellow was sitting outside it chewing tobacco as he cut up bacon with a large knife. A skillet lay at his feet and a small dog sniffed round waiting for scraps. The old man looked up without much interest when the marshal appeared.

'Is Clem around?' Eli asked without getting down from his horse.

'Still up at Kinnock Creek, like I told you last time you was asking,' the old man replied. 'Could

114

be gone some time. He's after gold.'

'Much chance of that?'

The old man grinned. 'A fella came tellin' us that he found near to two ounces up there last week. That's why I'm short of company right now.'

'Why ain't you with them? I took you for a prospector,' Eli said as he dismounted.

'Can't get around no more. Gone all rheumaticky. I just look after things for them and get food and lodgings. Could be worse.'

Eli nodded. 'Could be. Which is Clem's cabin?'

The old man pointed. 'That one, but you can't go in there. It wouldn't be right.'

Eli did not answer. He crossed to the wooden-planked hut with its turf roof and opened the door. A sour smell issued from the dark interior and the marshal pulled a wry face. As he put a foot across the earth floor, he heard a sudden noise behind him and half-turned. A large knife flew across the space between him and the old man. It buried itself in the door frame just a few inches from his shoulder.

The marshal swung clear and drew his gun as he turned to face the knife-thrower. He was already too late. The old man's legs had suddenly recovered from their rheumaticky condition and he was scurrying from sight behind the corrals. The small dog had jumped on the bacon slices and carried them away before any other scavangers could interfere.

Eli went into the hut and pulled the pieces of sacking away from the windows. He disturbed a few spiders and a roach, and loosened a curtain of dust. Sunlight poured into the little place and showed the small bunk, a wooden chest, and a rickety table on which stale food still provided a meal for a host of insects. There was nothing of interest in the chest or on the two shelves that housed candles and a couple of tin mugs. It was on the floor behind the bunk that he found what he was looking for.

There were six stone jars in a row, and next to them were four glass containers that held a pale-blue liquid. Two more empty glass jars had rolled under the bunk. They all bore labels of a chemical supplier in Chicago. Eli picked up one of the stone jars and took out the large cork. He sniffed the contents and pulled a face at the smell of Clem's corn mash. One of the other jars gave off the same aroma. It was the third container that had the marshal puzzled. The smell was acidy and something he had not come across before.

He picked up one of the glass jars and took a cautious sniff at its contents. It was the same acidy smell and the marshal stood puzzling over what he had found. A noise from outside suddenly drew his attention and he crossed to the window with one hand ready to draw his gun. The old prospector was back again. The gate of the corral had been opened and he was saddling the mule. Eli smiled a little as he went to the door and pointed the .44 at the man.

'Thinkin' of ridin' off to tell Clem I'm payin' him a visit?' he asked.

The old man stood with the large saddle in his two hands. His eyes flickered as he looked at the gun.

'I ain't armed,' he stuttered as he threw the saddle on the animal's back. 'You can't shoot a fella what ain't carryin' a gun.'

'Why not? You threw a knife at me when I had my back turned.'

'That was only to warn you off,' the old fellow protested. 'I didn't aim you should get hurt.'

'Well, that was sure considerate of you. Put the saddle back on the fence and come over here where we can have a little talk about your future.'

The old man made a move as if to obey. Then he suddenly shifted position so that the mule was between him and the gun. He grabbed the girth and tried to tighten it so that he could swing himself into the saddle. Eli Riley levelled the Colt carefully and pulled the trigger.

The saddle seemed to start rotating round the mule's back. The pommel hit the old man in the face as he let out a yell and dived for cover. The animal reared against the fence and then galloped off to the other end of the corral while the saddle fell to the ground. There was a neat hole in the worn leather.

Marshal Riley walked slowly over to the scene of action. He looked down at the old-timer and waved the gun playfully.

'You and me is gonna have a little talk,' he said, 'and then you're headin' out. But not to Kinnock Creek. If you did that, I might just meet you on the trail, and I wouldn't like that to happen. I'd either have to shoot you or take you back to town and a nice cold cell in my jailhouse. Do we understand each other?'

The old man picked himself up and nodded glumly.

'It weren't my doing,' he said humbly. 'It was them fellas what settled here after the creeks stopped pannin' anythin' over Clayton way. They joined up with old Clem and started work around these parts. Then them copper fellas messed things up with their diggin' and shovellin' teams. Nobody could make a livin' round here no more. And the folks in town didn't care. They was doin' well out it.'

'And somebody had the idea of poisonin' the creek that supplied the water to Murphy's Ford?'

The old man nodded eagerly. 'Yeah. One of them had used the same trick up north. So they got a few dollars together and had this chemical stuff sent to Fort Bracken by Wells Fargo. Clem picked it up from there. Then he tipped some into the creek every few days until folk in the town took sick. We didn't mean to hurt them. Just to make

118

trouble for the copper fellas. In case the town folk didn't think to blame the water, we told them about the creek bein' all discoloured near the mine workings. So old Doc Vale went out to check on it.'

'And who killed him?'

'I can't figure that. We certainly didn't, so don't go layin' the blame on us. We wanted him to tell folks about the poisonin' so that they'd blame the mine. His killin' was a damned shame. He was a decent fella.'

The marshal looked round at the few delapidated cabins.

'Yeah, he was. Well, you'd better be on your way, old-timer. And don't come back here. Folk in Murphy's Ford won't be any too friendly to you panhandlers when they hear what you did.'

The old man nodded eagerly and went back to harness his mule.

Eli Riley checked the other cabins but found nothing. Clem was clearly the leading light in the affair and the marshal set out for Kinnock Creek.

Kinnock Creek was the best part of a two-day journey. The ground rose steadily towards the distant hills and the heat drew a cloud of flies that surrounded the rider and his horse. Eli was sweating and tired when the wide, bubbling flush of water came into sight.

He stopped to fill his flask and let the horse

drink its fill. He knew from previous experience that the area worked by the gold-seekers was another mile or so towards the hills. Only the clumps of mesquite and the tall cactus bushes stopped him from being able to see the men at work. He could hear them. Voices carried over the still air and as the lawman neared the site of the gold-bearing area, he got his first view of the mass of ragged tents and hobbled mules that spread on either side of the creek.

There must have been well over thirty prospectors along the edges of the fast-flowing water. They worked like men possessed and nobody seemed to notice the arrival of a town marshal. Eli rode quietly along, trying to spot Clem among the dusty, streaked faces, which all bore a similar intensity as they spun the mud-laden water in their pans and ran their fingers through the deposit in the hope of striking it rich.

He eventually spotted the one he was looking for. The old man was up to his knees in the water and bending to fill the pan with another hope of wealth. The marshal got down from his horse and stood watching as the old prospector swirled the contents and then threw everything away in disgust.

'Not havin' much luck, Clem?' the marshal asked quietly.

The old prospector looked up and his eyes brightened for a moment. Then he noticed something that froze him. There was one of his stone jars tied to the cropper of the lawman's horse.

TWELVE

The riders got back to Murphy's Ford a few hours after Marshal Riley left to pick up old Clem. They were tired but triumphant. Their arrival was heralded by a rousing chorus of whoops and gunshots as they rode at a gallop down the main street. The whole town had to know how much damage they had done to the mining company.

Leo Ramsay watched from the window of his bank. He chewed the ends of his sideburns nervously and shook his head as he heard glass breaking in the windows of some of the stores that supported the copper company. The Hadley House already had the windows boarded up or that would also have been a victim of the excitement. Young Jim Hadley was with his father round at the feed-store office. He looked with contempt at the cowering mayor behind the desk.

'You should never have let Eli Riley leave town,' he snapped. 'He's the only one who can deal with these people. They're goin' to wreck the place once they get loose in the saloons.'

'What the hell could I do?' Bert Hadley whined. 'I was hopin' that if he brought that damned old fool back here and threw him in the jailhouse, folk would realize that the minin' company had nothin' to do with poisonin' the water. Surely they can see that?'

'It's Doc Vale and his wife they're mad about, as well you know, Pa.'

'I never forget that for one moment. But it's over and done with. The town is more important than anythin' else. We all need it.'

The young hotel manager snorted.

'Well, I reckon Murphy's Ford is finished. I haven't got a single payin' customer at the hotel. The place is empty. And until we get some glass in the windows and the town cools down, nobody is goin' to be takin' rooms with us. Where are those damned deputies anyway?'

The mayor shrugged hopelessly. 'Ed and Sid have vanished,' he said sadly. 'You'd think your own kin would be there when they're needed, but I'll lay odds they're a dozen miles away and headin' for some place safe.'

Jim Hadley suddenly clicked his fingers and a slight smile came to his thin features.

'We've got just the man in the jailhouse,' he said. 'Young Tom Vale was a lawman, and he's said to be one hell of a gun-handler. Why not deputize him? Those folk won't argue with a fella like that when it comes to shooting. And remember, Pa, he's on their side in this copper-mine business. He'll quieten the town in no time flat. Turn him loose on them.'

The mayor thought about it for a moment. Then he nodded his head vigorously.

'I think you got a good idea, son,' he said a little more cheerfully. 'I'll go down to the jailhouse and have a word with him.'

Tom Vale sat behind the marshal's desk. His deputy's badge was pinned on a newly bought shirt and a gun was at his side. The mayor had been surprised to find that Tom had not been locked in his cell. But it did make things easier and the young man eyed the mayor shrewdly as the offer was made, He accepted the job of deputy with a wry smile. It was the easiest way of staying in town, And he needed to be in Murphy's Ford until justice was done.

He looked at the clock on the opposite wall. It was dark outside now and folk were taking their evening meal. His presence on the main street a couple of hours earlier had calmed things down. He did not have to make any gesture of authority. He merely walked around, talking to folk and listening to the tales of daring along the railroad line. He suggested quietly that they must all be tired and hungry. Joining their families would be a good thing, and even the excitable Peter Murphy had gone home without argument.

The trouble would come when they had all rested and then headed off for the saloons. He knew that he would have to pay attention to the Palomino rather than to the more sedate Golden Globe. Another couple of hours and the alcohol would begin to take effect.

It began just after midnight. Tom had made a patrol only half an hour earlier. The Palomino was noisy and he had to break up a fight between a couple of drunks. He felt that his presence and prompt action had calmed things down and went back to the jailhouse for a cup of coffee.

He almost dropped the tin mug when the door flew open and Preacher Edwards came panting into the office.

'We've got real trouble, Tom,' he gasped. 'There's a mob round at the mayor's place. They're going to burn it down.'

'The Hadley House?' Tom Vale jumped to his feet and crossed to the gun rack.

'No. They're heading round to the feed store,' the preacher said tensely. 'Little Arnie Martin tells me that the only reason they're not going for the hotel is because it's too close to other buildings. They reckon that the feed store is a safer place to attack. Can you stop them, lad? I'll do all I can to help.'

The two men hurried from the jailhouse and along the street to the lane that led to the feed store. There were plenty of people about and they were all heading in the same direction. The crowd was noisy and a few stones were thrown at the upper windows of the hotel as they passed it. Tom noticed that there were no lights on in the building and guessed that the family would be sheltering somewhere in their living quarters. He nursed the shotgun under his arm and cursed the damage to his left hand that made things so difficult for him. He was still in pain and the fingers seemed to be almost frozen and tingling in an odd way.

He noticed that some of the excited men were carrying oil lamps and bundles of rags. The preacher was already lagging behind, partly because of his age, and partly, the deputy suspected, because of a feeling of hopelessness. Tom had a sudden idea and cut down one of the lanes. He came out at the back of the Palomino saloon and, although out of breath, did what he had to do. He then ran back to the main street with something approaching a grin on his face. The preacher was waiting for him, unhappy to go on alone to see what was happening at the feed store. The two men joined up again just as the mob was beginning to break into the building.

Tom drew his gun and fired a single shot into the air. There was a sudden hush as everything stopped and all the angry faces turned to look at the newly appointed deputy with the preacher at his side.

126

'I don't like the copper fellas any more than you do,' Tom Vale shouted, 'but I like this town, and I sure don't fancy the idea of folk burnin' it down. You owe it to my ma and pa and to your own families to make a decent life here. And why in hell did you start settin' the Palomino alight? If that fire spreads. . . !'

He did not have to say any more. All interest in the feed store was finished as the crowd of horror-struck men turned back the way they had come to rescue the most treasured building in Murphy's Ford, The deputy marshal watched them go with a quiet smile on his face. Preacher Edwards threw him a thankful glance.

'That was well handled, Tom,' he said. 'Nobody hurt and nobody blamed. Very well done, lad. But what's going to happen when they find that their saloon is not on fire?'

The young deputy grinned. 'I don't go around tellin' lies, Reverend,' he said softly. 'The Palomino needs quite a few pails of water throwin' over its back fences. I set light to some straw in the corral and piled a bit of it along the stoop. That'll keep them busy until the excitement wears off. I don't think they'll be back here tonight, and by tomorrow they'll all have come to their senses. Let's go have a cup of coffee.'

Tom was right. The town quietened down and only the abandoned oil lamps and the smell of burning remained. A few rags littered the main street and two of the water troughs were nearly empty. But Murphy's Ford was at peace and the new deputy eventually managed to get some sleep.

The stores were a bit late opening the next morning but the children went off to school at the usual time and with the usual reluctance. The mayor ventured out a little hesitantly to visit his feed store. Nobody seemed to be looking at him with any bitterness as he saluted the ladies, nodded to the men, and climbed the rickety steps to his office feeling slightly safer.

His son was supervising the replacement of the glass in the hotel windows while Tom Vale went off to the home of his parents. He still had to sort everything out there. He wandered a little aimlessly around the silent house. He was not quite sure what to do with all the furniture and piles of books that had been gathered over the years. It was while he was clearing out a bundle of medical journals that a loud knock on the front door interrupted him. He opened it to find one of the local store owners just raising his fist for another agitated knock.

'Tom, if you're still the deputy marshal, I reckon this is your problem,' the man stuttered. 'The bank ain't open and the clerks can't get no answer from Leo Ramsay's house. You'd better come along, fella.'

The young deputy wearily followed the worried

man down the lane and on to the main street. There were at least half a dozen people outside the closed bank and one of the clerks was trying to pacify them.

'He's not skipped town,' Tom heard the man telling them. 'Mr Ramsay ain't that sorta fella. He's an honest man. Just wait patient, folks, and either he'll be here in a coupla minutes, or Simon will be back with the keys.'

'Ain't he got a wife and family?' the deputy asked the man at his side.

'No, she died a few years back. He has a daughter but she's married to some fella up Tucson way. Here comes old Simon now and he don't seem to have the keys.'

An elderly clerk had come out of one of the lanes and was hurrying back to the bank. He changed direction slightly when he caught sight of the deputy and hurried across to him.

'There's somethin' wrong back there,' he said as he gasped for breath. 'I can't get an answer and the curtains are drawn over the windows. I think Mr Ramsay must have taken ill. We'll have to break in.'

'Has he a horse?' the deputy asked as he looked up and down the street to see if any help was coming in the shape of the mayor or the judge.

'Yes, and it's in the corral at the back of the house. Along with his rig. He ain't left town, if that's what people is thinking.'

'You help pacify them folks at the bank. I'll go and see what I can do back there.'

The little clerk hurried to join his colleague and the impatient customers while Tom walked slowly and reluctantly to do his duty. The banker's house was in a quiet lane among three other homes of prominent citizens. There were trees and a small garden with white fences and an iron gate. He walked up the gravelled path and tried the front door. It was a hopeless gesture and a waste of time. He walked round the back and did the same thing against the solid bulk of the rear door.

'I figure as how you'll have to use your boot.'

The voice startled him and he turned to find the judge leaning over his own garden fence with a cigar in his mouth.

'Mornin' to you, Judge,' Tom greeted the old man. 'Any idea what's happened here?'

'No, but that clerk fella knockin' and hollerin' was enough to make my wife real curious. She tried peekin' through the windows but them curtains is too thick and she's as mad as a hungry coyote. So I gotta find out. Want to borrow a hammer?'

'I think I'll need one.'

The door soon gave way after a couple of sharp blows against the lock. Tom Vale entered a little fearfully and was comforted to know that the old judge was just behind him. The smell of the cigar was strong in the warm air of the kitchen. There was no sign of life and the stove was not lit. The two men moved through to the living room and looked around in the dimness caused by the drawn curtains. Tom went across and pulled them apart. The sunlight flooded in and then they saw a sight that made them both swear more in astonishment than horror.

A body lay in the middle of the floor. It was belly down on the Turkey carpet and the semi-bald head bore a gash from a single blow. Blood had congealed all around and the man's face was turned towards the intruders. The eyes were slightly open and the features, clean shaven and pale, were of somebody in middle age.

'Who the hell is it?' Tom asked. 'It certainly ain't Leo Ramsay but I can't claim to know all the folk in Murphy's Ford yet.'

The judge stood over the body and thoughtfully dropped ash on the carpet.

'Complete stranger,' he said softly, 'but did you ever see such a sight in your life, lad?'

Tom nodded.

'I know what you mean, Judge,' he said softly. 'What the hell are folks goin' to say when we go out there and tell them that the fella is wearin' no clothes?'

THIRTEEN

Marshal Riley arrived back in Murphy's Ford in the late afternoon. He and old Clem had travelled slowly. The prospector's mule delayed them by its slow pace and desire to stop at every succulent plant to satisfy a voracious appetite. Clem was not in a hurry to end the journey either. He barely spoke and kept spitting out the chewed tobacco as if disgusted with the world around him.

Eli Riley was glad to reach the main street. The quietness of the place surprised him, and as he pulled rein at the jailhouse, he was accosted by a shout from across the street. It was Ezra Davis standing on the steps of his pharmacy. The marshal dismounted and waited for the man to join him.

'What's the matter round here, Ezra?' he asked as he helped Clem climb down from the mule. 'Haven't them fellas returned from attackin' the railroad yet?'

'Oh, they're back all right, Marshal,' the pharmacist told him. 'But we got far worse happenin' in town right now. It's the bank. There ain't a bent cent in the whole place. Leo Ramsay cleared it out and left town.'

The marshal opened his mouth to say something but merely shook his head in disbelief. It was Clem who brightened up. He spat out a stream of juice and gave vent to a loud chuckle.

'Best news I've heard today.' He grinned. 'And it all happened while you was away scarin' the guts out of a poor old fella like me.'

Ezra Davis told the rest of the story and the lawman listened with greater disbelief as he heard of the unknown naked man and the discovery of something else even more important.

He thanked the man and began to lead Clem into the jailhouse. Then a thought occured to him and he took the old prospector by the arm.

'Let's go along to Leo's house,' he said quietly. 'The judge had the sense to leave the body where it fell until I got back, so maybe an old-timer like you can put a name to it.'

'Willin' to try,' Clem said cheerfully. 'Ain't had so much fun since my wife left me.'

The house of the banker was still guarded by the mayor and Judge Lester. They sat on the stoop, smoking their cigars and with a few children watching from beyond the picket fence. They both looked relieved to see the marshal arrive on the scene.

'Well, now. We've been waitin' for you. You're really a sight for sore eyes,' the judge called out cheerfully. 'Leo Ramsay has raided his own bank, killed some fella who might have been his partner, and now departed for distant shores. Come and take a look.'

They trooped into the house and the marshal looked down at the corpse with a puzzled expression on his face.

'Why take all his clothes?' he asked.

'Leo needed them,' the judge said shrewdly. 'This fella must have had a horse and Leo used it to get away. He also needed clothes that wouldn't label him the most dazzlin' dresser in the territory.'

'And the keys of the bank?'

'Left on that table. He emptied everything out and came back here to change and light out before the town woke up. But that ain't all, Tom. Look what's over there.'

The judge pointed to the large collection of guns and swords that decorated one wall of the well-furnished room. They formed a history of American warfare, and were the hobby of the missing banker. Some cynical folk felt that he used them to emphasize his own heroism in the paymaster's department.

A Spencer carbine occupied a space on a rack that held several other guns. The marshal took it down and smelt the barrel. There was a slight hint of burnt powder. He opened the breech and scratched with his fingernail.

'I'll let Phineas Hoffman take a look at this,' he said, 'but my guess is that this has been fired a short time ago.'

'There are two cartridges in the desk drawer,' the judge said grimly.

Eli glanced at the two men before pulling open the drawer indicated and taking out the bullets. He stood weighing them in his hand, then suddenly turned to the old prospector.

'Do you know him, Clem?' he asked.

'Can't say as I do,' the old man answered quietly. 'Sure ain't one of the local villains. You'll have to take a look at your wanted lists, Marshal. There may be a reward for him, but there sure ain't for me.'

'There is one chance,' the mayor said in a quiet voice. 'Young Tom Vale has gone after him.'

The marshal looked from one to the other of the two men.

'I was keepin' him outa trouble,' he said wearily. 'That young fella has a habit of tearin' away like a hungry coyote. What the hell's he got to do with anythin' like this?'

The mayor had to explain about making him a deputy marshal.

'And that gun confirmed who killed his folks,' he pointed out grimly. 'I could hardly stop him goin' after Leo Ramsay, now could I? You weren't here and the folks would expect it.'

'I suppose you didn't think to take a look in Tom Vale's saddlebags before he left town?' the marshal asked.

There was a long silence and it was the judge who eventually broke. His gravelly voice was hesitant.

'Are you suggestin' that the young fella was carryin' the bank's money?' he asked.

'Could be,' Eli told him with a certain relish. 'You make a known gunslinger your deputy marshal. Then you let him leave town after the bank has been robbed. Ain't that just a little careless?'

'But the clothes, and the carbine?' the mayor protested. 'And where in hell is Leo Ramsay?'

'Leo could have been his partner along with this fella. They could have planned it carefully for days. I think you can say a farewell to your deputy and your money now. Let's get this one under ground before the house becomes as smelly as Clem's place.'

Phineas Hoffman confirmed that the Spencer carbine had been recently fired and nobody had bothered to clean it. It now sat in the marshal's office while he occupied the desk after a welcome meal at home with his long-suffering but ever patient wife. It was dark outside and the oil lamp on the ceiling threw a warm glow over the quiet jailhouse. Clem was safely tucked away in a cell and the marshal was on the point of deciding to return home and have a long and well-deserved rest. He had carefully searched the banker's house and then taken the keys to visit the bank. There were things he had to think about.

It was as he was reaching to extinguish the lamp that Clem suddenly seemed to awaken.

'Don't put that light out, Marshal,' the old man shouted urgently.

'You scared of the dark, Clem?'

'Hell, no. But I reckon you and me has got some talkin' to do.'

The marshal walked over to the bars and looked at the old fellow sitting upright on the bunk.

'What have you got to tell me, Clem?' he asked quietly.

There was a sly look in the watery eyes of the old panhandler.

'This business of puttin' stuff in the creek,' Clem said slowly. 'We didn't mean no real harm and we sure as hell never meant to poison folks. They was just ill for a few days, and us prospectors got a chance to put one over on them minin' fcllas. We was desperate, Marshal. Real desperate.'

'You've said all that before, Clem, and I'm sure the judge will be reasonable. I'll speak up for you, but understand this, old fella, what you did started off all the trouble we got now. It cost the lives of Doc Vale and his wife. Folk won't forget that. Even if the judge goes easy on you, how do you think the town will feel when they hear all the details. You'll be lucky to avoid a lynchin' if they get their hands on you.'

'Yeah. I know. That's why I'm ready to make a deal. I want outa this town.'

Eli Riley looked hard at the shifty eyes of the old rogue. 'What sorta deal do you think you could make, Clem?' he asked.

'I could give you the name of that dead fella in Leo Ramsay's house.'

FOURTEEN

There were no mourners at the funeral of the unknown man. The preacher did his job with considerable humanity, but he spoke the words only to the grave-diggers and the mortician. Nobody wanted to be seen associating in any way with what had happened at the bank.

The wealthier men of the town had all loaned a few dollars each to keep the bank open and doing business until money could arrive by the weekly stage. The mining company had not offered any help. Ross Kimber made it clear that Murphy's Ford was no longer going to be supported by him. The mayor was deep in thought as he stood at the top of the steps of his feed store and watched what was happening.

The burial ground was on the edge of town and he could see what was going on there from his elevated position. His reverie was interrupted by the arrival of Marshal Riley. The lawman stumped heavily up the wooden steps and leaned against the rail next to the mayor.

'Not the best attended of funerals,' Eli said with a nod in the direction of the event.

'You seem to be happy enough about it,' the mayor snapped angrily. 'This town is in trouble and I would have thought that our lawman might at least be out there lookin' for the thieves. Tom Vale and Leo Ramsay must be laughin' themselves silly by now.'

'I was wrong about Tom,' Eli admitted quietly. 'I figure as how he'll be comin' back to town in the next day or so.'

The mayor blinked. 'But you said—'

'I know what I said, and I was wrong. Tom's as honest a fella as you could wish to meet. He'll be back here as soon as he finds that he has no trail to follow.'

'Then what is happenin' in this town, Eli? And who in hell is the dead man?'

The marshal grinned. 'Oh, I can put a name to him easily enough. They've just buried Leo Ramsay.'

There was a long silence while the mayor absorbed the news.

'You seem to have been drinkin' some of Clem's corn mash,' he said at last, in a low voice. 'I've known Leo for years, and that fella in the house was as bald as a. . . .'

His words faded away as he saw the grin on the lawman's weather-beaten face.

140

'You're right,' the marshal said. 'Leo had a fine head of hair and the choicest set of sidewhiskers that ever took root. But there were a few scratches round the chin of that dead body. The sorta little nicks you make when you shave in a hurry. Then I had a look at Leo's bowl and razor. They was still wet. And there's another little thing about our late moneylender. He wore a wig.'

'I never knew that,' the mayor muttered.

'He didn't want us to know about it. But he lost his hair all sudden-like durin' the war. Nasty folk would say that he got too near the action at one time and scared himself silly. They got a fancy name for it, but I ain't no medical man.'

'So you're tellin' me that somebody killed Leo, took his keys, and emptied the bank?'

'That's right. And then tried to make it look like Leo was the thief and had killed his partner before leavin' town. But there was no partner and Leo never left town.'

The mayor drummed his fingers nervously on the wooden rail.

'Are you sure about all this?' he asked.

'Sure as sure. You see, Leo was proud of that collection of guns. I'd looked at it a few times, and I never did see a Spencer carbine in the collection. And when I checked his desk at the bank, the pair of Army Colts were still there. He wouldn't leave town without those two treasures. They meant a lot to him.'

141

'I see what you mean,' the mayor said in a small voice. 'So the carbine was put there to blame him for the Vale killings?'

'Yes. So, as I say, Tom Vale will be comin' back to Murphy's Ford still lookin' for the killer. And that fella must be in town. And he has all the bank's money to enjoy until your hot-headed young deputy catches up with him.'

The mayor looked round despairingly.

'Have you any idea who's behind all this, Eli?' he asked.

'Nope. It could be just about anybody who wanted to save the copper minin' company or who wanted to rob the bank. Could be two entirely different fellas we're after. I just don't know.'

'Well, you've sure found out a few things, and I'm sorry about bitin' your head off. But we still got problems, Eli. Real nasty problems.'

'Mayor, you don't know the half of it. This town could explode any minute and I got no deputies.'

Clem had finished his supper and wiped the plate clean with a large piece of Ma Riley's bread. He drank his coffee noisily and then lay back on the bunk with a chew of tobacco in his mouth. The marshal came across and looked at him through the bars.

'I got some bad news for you, Clem,' he said with a grin. 'You can't stay here no longer enjoyin' my wife's cookin' and livin' like a kept floozy. You

142

gotta go back home.'

The old man rose from the bunk and crossed over to the bars.

'I ain't in no particular hurry,' he said, 'but it sounds as if what I told you about Leo Ramsay has been useful. What did the mayor say when he heard about the wig?'

'He thought I was one very clever town marshal,' Eli told him happily.

'I reckon as how you played it smart, then. And don't worry. I ain't a talkative sorta fella. But why the hurry to see the back of me?'

The lawman became serious. 'This town is like a powder barrel, Clem,' he said grimly. 'There are folk here still stirrin' up trouble and I don't want you to be lynched.'

The old man gulped. 'Yeah, I was afraid of that. When do I leave?'

'As soon as the town quiets down for the night. I'll get your mule ready and you can head for Kinnock Creek. Don't go back to your cabin till things are sorted out here. Tom Vale is due back soon and I figure as how what I have to tell him will keep this town more worried about his gunslingin' than about a few old panhandlers spoilin' the water supply.'

Clem left Murphy's Ford soon after midnight. The marshal watched him heading north and smiled at the thought that it was the first time he had seen the old man without a corn-mash jar tied to his saddle. When the prospector was safely out of sight the lawman made one last patrol of the town before turning in for the night. The Golden Globe was nearly empty but the Palomino's noise still blared out into the street. Eli peered over the swing doors and noted the various groupings at the bar. Peter Murphy was there, his voice louder than the rest. The marshal turned away. He knew that it would take weeks for the message to sink in with folk like Peter Murphy. The town had lost any chance of growing and the raucous bellowings of the storekeeper were helping to make things worse.

He turned away and began to walk back to the jailhouse. There was a sudden shout behind him and the marshal looked to see what was going on. Peter Murphy stood in the middle of the street. He swayed slightly as he approached the lawman but the whiskey was giving him courage. His admiring friends were coming out of the saloon, equally fuelled but keeping well to the rear.

'We hear tell you got old Clem in the jailhouse,' the storekeeper shouted challengingly. 'It's the copper fellas that should be there.'

The marshal decided to bluff it out, although there must have been twenty or more men outside the Palomino by now. He walked slowly towards Peter Murphy to stare him straight in the eyes.

'Clem and his partners put stuff in the creek so

that the copper company would be blamed,' he said in a voice that carried to everyone on the street. 'They didn't aim to hurt anyone and there are somethin' like a dozen old panhandlers involved. The copper company had nothin' to do with it. But you went wild and pulled up the railroad tracks. You've killed this town as sure as Washington crossed the Delaware. Right now, fella, you need to talk in a low voice.'

There was a silence in the crowd and the marshal spat on the ground in front of the storekeeper to show his public contempt. All support for Peter Murphy suddenly seemed to vanish and some of the drinkers even backed away and began to sidle into the saloon again. The lawman knew that he had won and turned away with a sigh of content.

There was a sudden yell of warning and Eli Riley spun round to face the crowd again. Peter Murphy held a Colt .44 in his right hand. He had snatched it from the holster of the nearest man and now waved it menacingly at the marshal.

'Put that away, fella,' Eli warned as his hand slid down towards the butt of his own gun. 'We don't want any more trouble in this town. There's been enough killin' already.'

'You ain't such a big man now,' the storekeeper shouted. 'You fellas with guns think you rule us ordinary folk. Well, I've got a gun now and I ain't afraid to use it. If that Clem fella poisoned the water for our kids, I reckon we gotta do somethin' about it.'

'Nobody's gettin' lynched in my town,' Eli snapped. 'Put that gun away and go home to your family. Those fellas behind you ain't on your side any more. You're on your own now.'

The man hesitated for a moment and cast a hurried glance at those who had followed him. There were fewer now and they appeared to be merely spectators. For one brief moment he seemed about to do what the marshal ordered. Then his drunken pride took over and he pulled back the hammer as he swung the gun at the lawman.

Eli drew his own Colt, and as he pulled the trigger, he felt the heavy blow of a bullet hitting him somewhere on his right side. His own cartridge found a fatal mark. Peter Murphy stumbled back with a ludicrous expression of surprise on his face as the blood oozed slowly from his chest. He collapsed in a heap on the ground and the gun slipped from his dying hand.

The marshal stood and watched. He was afraid to look down at his own body. There was some pain but he did not feel that he was seriously injured. He turned to the crowd and asked someone to call the pharmacist to see if anything could be done for the fallen man. Even as he spoke, Peter Murphy died and somebody went for the mortician instead.

146

Eli turned away, holstered the gun, and massaged his right hip with a shaking hand. He suddenly realized that there was no blood. He looked down and almost let out a whoop of delight when he found that the storekeeper's bullet had hit his belt. The row of ammunition stored there had taken the blow. The cartridge cases were intact but the lead bullets were broken off almost where they fitted into the casings. Peter Murphy's shot had been deflected and all the marshal had suffered was a bruised hip.

He went back to the jailhouse and locked up for the night. He had no wish to see the mayor or any other worthy of the town. His hand was still trembling and all that he wanted was to get home to his wife. He even smiled at the prospect. It was many years since he had been so anxious for her company.

He trudged wearily homeward. His thoughts were on the happenings in the town over such a short period. And then an idea struck him that stopped the marshal in his tracks. He stood in the side lane cursing his own stupidity. The first man he had to see in the morning was Phineas Hoffman.

FIFTEEN

Young Milly Hoffman was brushing the stoop when Marshal Riley arrived. It was early morning, with the children on their way to school and the businesses just beginning to open. She looked at the lawman in surprise when he entered the gun store and took her pa by the arm for what seemed to be a confidential talk.

'Phineas, I've been doin' some real hard thinkin' about the killin' of the Vales,' Eli said urgently. 'I shoulda cottoned on to it earlier, but I guess I was too dumb.'

'So what's the problem?' the gunsmith asked as he led the way through to the living quarters. His wife greeted the two of them with a smiling nod and began to pour out coffee. The breakfast things were still on the table and she had been clearing them away.

'Well, the idea of killin' Doc Vale could only have been thought up just a few days before it happened. And the fella what did the killin' had no real store of guns that he could use. He was somebody who never needed a rifle or carbine. He only had an old piece from the war. Somethin' that hadn't been used in years and was just lyin' around with no ammunition. That's when them bullets were stolen from your store. He might own a pistol or a shotgun, but nothin' for a long shot that had to be accurate. See what I mean?'

The big gunsmith nodded soberly. 'You're right,' he said slowly. 'So he came to my store just a few days before the killing?'

'That's it. So who did you have in the store in those few days that wasn't a regular customer and who was left alone while you went into the workshop or came back here?'

The storekeeper sat down heavily in one of the chairs and drank his coffee slowly. The silence was tense while the marshal and Ma Hoffman watched him.'

'There was a fella,' he said at last, in a rather uncertain voice. 'Came in one mornin' with a shotgun. Said that he'd forgotten to clean it last time he went out after jackrabbits. The thing was real bad and I went through to the workshop and left him alone in the store for quite a time. But it couldn't be him, Eli. Not him.'

'What's his name, Phineas?' The marshal's voice was urgent.

The gunsmith told him.

Marshal Riley walked slowly back to the jailhouse. He was still limping despite the treatment meted out by the pharmacist. Swabbing his bruised hip with arnica had not helped very much and his gunbelt was rubbing against the swelling. He knew now what had happened and who was responsible. There was a job to be done and it was not one that he relished.

There was a horse at the rail when he arrived. Tom Vale had returned to town.

The young man was in the office, lighting the stove and looking tired and dusty. He managed a slight smile when the lawman entered and put the coffee pot on to boil.

'Glad to see you, Marshal,' Tom said thankfully. 'I guess the mayor's told you about me chasin' after the folk that killed Leo Ramsay?'

'He did. And about you bein' made a deputy. You came back because you couldn't find a trail. Am I right?'

The young man looked surprised.

'How did you guess? Am I that obvious a green-horn?'

The marshal crossed to his chair and sat down carefully. He started to tell the story, hesitating in parts and massaging his hip as he spoke. Tom Vale listened in stunned surprise and his face hardened when the killer of his parents was finally named.

The coffee was forgotten until the pot bubbled over and the steam drew the attention of the two men.

'And I suppose I'm to sit quiet while you do the arrestin' and Judge Lester and twelve other local drunks decide about the hanging?'

The young man's words were bitter and hostile.

'That's the law,' Marshal Riley said quietly.

'Well, I don't go for law,' Tom Vale spat angrily. 'I go for justice, and I aim to get it for myself.'

The marshal rose from his chair and went across to the stove.

'Funnily enough, fella,' he said slowly, 'I don't go a lot for law myself. The old judge sticks to the rules like they was some sorta sacred writin' from Holy Scripture. Lawyers is like that. They always put law before justice and you never hear them say that the law is wrong. It just ain't in their nature.'

He poured himself a cup of coffee and warmed his hands on the tin mug. His eyes never left the other man's face.

'But law's a thing that cuts two ways, son,' he said. 'The mayor deputized you, and now you're the law. If I order you to go and arrest the fella what killed your folks, you'd have to carry out my orders.'

Tom's face lightened as he saw the hint of a grin from the marshal. He nodded silently.

'So I'm sendin' you out to arrest a killer. Phineas

Hoffman tells me that the fella owns a shotgun and a short-barrelled Colt. If he chooses to make a fight of it, you might have to kill him. It would be a pity, but these things happen, don't they?'

Tom Vale nodded silently and checked the Colt at his side. He looked at the shotguns in the wall rack but decided not to take one. The marshal watched from the stoop as the young man walked slowly down the main street and entered the door of the Hadley House hotel.

There were no guests and the clerk behind the desk was despondently dusting the polished mahogany. He looked up with surprise at the appearance of the deputy and stood watching vacantly as the young man crossed to the living quarters of the Hadley family at the back of the building.

Ma Hadley sat in a wing chair near the window and was doing some sewing. She looked up in alarm as the door flew open and outlined the lawman who stood like some menacing avenger.

'Where's your son?'

The words were hardly spoken when a door was heard being slammed somewhere close. Tom Vale ran to the window where Ma Hadley sat. It overlooked the corral at the rear of the hotel and Jim Hadley was already opening the gate and reaching for the saddle that lay across the fence. He flung it across the horse's back and began reaching for the girth. The deputy ran out of the room and along the narrow corridor to the kitchen. The rear door was the one he had heard close. He threw it open and drew his gun.

A shot blasted his ears and the door shook in his hand as a bullet tore off a splintered strip of wood. The deputy fired at the man who was now running round behind the roan mare, which was beginning to move in its fright at the noise. Tom's shot went wide and he cocked the gun again to try and get a better aim at his opponent. Then it all went wrong. Something hit him across the back of the head and he stumbled to his knees. He did not lose consciousness but blood poured down over his face and the Colt fell from his limp grip. He felt sick and dizzy and was vaguely aware of a woman running past him.

Ma Hadley helped her son to saddle and bridle the mare. She hugged him and then held the gate open while he rode out of the corral and down the lane towards the edge of town.

And that was where Marshal Riley was waiting. The big lawman stepped out with a shotgun raised to his shoulder. Jim Hadley heard his order to stop but dug his heels desperately into the flanks of the animal. He held the rein in his left hand and reached for the gun to kill the marshal. The shotgun blasted once and the young fugitive fell backwards from the saddle and slithered to the ground with his head blown away. The marshal had deliberately fired high to spare the horse.

Eli Riley walked the animal back to the corral and closed the gate on it. People were gathering in the lane but he ignored them. He went to the back door of the hotel and smiled gently as he watched his deputy leaning against the wall and trying to wipe the blood off his face.

'Was that Ma Hadley's doing?' he asked.

The young man nodded. 'She hit me with a skillet,' he said ruefully, 'and then apologized when young Jim took off. I figure as how she's gone to the feed store now to break the news to the mayor.'

'I'm goin' along there to see him myself,' the marshal said drily. 'You go have a word with the pharmacist.'

Eli Riley went into the hotel and was passing the door of the living room when he realized that Ma Hadley was sitting by the window. She was quietly sobbing and looked up when she heard the marshal's footsteps.

'I didn't mean to hurt young Tom,' she said tearfully, 'but Jim is my son, and I had to try and help him escape, bad as he and his pa may be. You understand, Eli?'

The marshal nodded sympathetically and went through to the foyer. The clerk was not there and the whole place had a weirdly deserted look about it. He stepped out onto the main street and walked round to the feed store. The rickety stairs warned the mayor of his approach and the First Citizen had already risen from his desk when the lawman entered.

'I heard the shooting,' he said in an agitated voice. 'What's been happenin' in town, Eli?'

'The man who killed the Vales has just been shot. He was tryin' to get away.'

The mayor went pale. His mouth opened but no words came out. He went back to the desk and sat down heavily.

'My son,' he whispered sadly. 'You've come to tell me that Jim is dead.'

'That's right. Suppose you start bein' honest about it, Bert.'

'I didn't know what he did until after the Spencer carbine was mentioned,' the mayor said in what was almost a whisper. 'When Doc Vale came to tell me about the poisonin' of the water, I naturally talked about it at home. I knew that once word got out, the folk in this town would turn on the copper company. Just like they did. We'd be ruined. Young Jim took it real hard. His future was in that hotel and I reckon he didn't want the doc comin' back here and tellin' us that the copper folk were poisonin' the water. That old gun had been been lyin' around the place since the end of the war. He must have ridden out and killed Doc Vale.'

'He did,' the marshal said drily, 'and then he came back here to silence Ma Vale as well. If the doc had never talked to that old fool Morton, we'd never have known why the killings took place.'

The mayor nodded sadly. 'I couldn't give him away, Eli,' he said. 'You know how a father feels. You're a good marshal and you worked it all out. Bess and I will have to leave town now. Our days here are over.'

'There's still the bank robbery and the killin' of Leo Ramsay,' the lawman said.

'Oh, you'll solve that sooner or later,' the mayor told him confidently.

'I already have solved it. You forget that your Spencer was left at Leo's house. And so were the rest of the stolen bullets. Your son did that as well.'

The mayor sighed and went back to his desk. He sat down and opened a drawer to take out a couple of glasses.

'Yes, I can see that now,' he murmured.

'So that just leaves us with one question, Bert,' the lawman said. 'Where is the bank's money?'

The hand holding the glasses trembled.

'I imagine he's hidden it some place,' the mayor muttered.

'I reckon he has. There's a safe at the hotel, but your clerk uses that in the course of his duties. Then you've got another safe right here in this office. You never have to open that with other folk around. So open it now.'

The mayor dropped the glasses on to the desk.

One of them rolled off and smashed on the floor.

'Are you accusing me. . . ?'

'Who else could plan it all? Open the safe.'

The First Citizen got up from the chair. He took a couple of steps towards the small green safe and then turned back.

'The keys are in the desk,' he said in a low voice.

He opened the top left-hand drawer and reached inside. When he withdrew his hand, it was clutching a double-barrelled derringer. He swung it round at the marshal and pulled back the hammer. He was too late: the lawman's gun was drawn and cocked before the mayor realized that his action had been anticipated. The shot took him in the chest and he reeled against the wall before collapsing in front of the safe.

Marshal Riley pulled open the drawer of the desk a little further and took out a small bunch of keys. He moved the body slightly and started trying them in the safe lock. His fourth attempt gave the result he wanted. When he opened the safe, the bank's money was a welcome sight to see.

The marshal's office was warm and the two men sat drinking whiskey to celebrate the day's work. Young Tom Vale had a bandage round his head but appeared cheerful and alert. The marshal was still aching and kept rubbing his hip as he changed position on the chair.

'The arnica ain't workin' then?' Tom asked cheekily.

'No, it ain't, and it's at times like this that we miss your pa,' the marshal said with a rueful grin.

'Let me take a look at the damage,' the young man suggested. 'I might be able to help.'

Eli Riley hesitated for a moment, then got out of the chair and pulled up his shirt while he lowered his pants slightly. Tom touched the purplish flesh and gave vent to a slight whistle.

'That's more than just a bruise,' he said. 'The vessels have burst under the skin and a large clot of blood has formed. When you've had a few more whiskeys, we'll go along to my pa's surgery and I'll cut it out. You'll be as frisky as a new-born colt in a coupla days.'

The marshal covered himself up again and looked hard at the young man.

'I know that the whiskey goes down well, fella, but are you sure you know what you're doing?' he asked.

Tom grinned. 'My pa sent me north to study medicine. The gunslingin' was my idea of enjoyin' life before settlin' down to curin' warts and deliverin' babies. I wouldn't say no to stayin' in this town and takin' up where Pa left off. If they'll have me.'

The marshal grinned. 'I reckon they'll have you all right,' he said happily, 'but I won't put your name forward until I see how you turn out on this business of mine. Now, I'll do the drinkin' and you do the

158

stayin' sober. You're gonna need a steady hand.'

As the lawman poured himself another glass of whiskey, the door flew open and the judge appeared. His eyes lit up at the sight of the bottle and he took a seat to join in.

'I've told the council all about the Hadleys,' he said as he sipped his drink. 'And I reckon you two fellas are the heroes of the hour. I just got one problem with you, Marshal. You let old Clem go free. Now that ain't right, nohow. He and his prospector friends poisoned the water supply of Murphy's Ford. He's gotta be brought to trial and you had no authority to release him.'

'I had to let him go, Judge,' the marshal said firmly. 'The folk in this town were gonna lynch him. I had no deputies and no backin' from the mayor or from you. If I hadn't let him go, we'd have had another killin' in Murphy's Ford. So let's just forget Clem. He's too old to send to jail, and so are most of the fellas who live in that old minin' camp with him.'

The judge grimaced and held out his glass.

'Well, I hope you at least got rid of all them chemicals he was usin' up there,' he growled in one last attempt to stress his authority.

The marshal grinned.

'Oh, I did that. I dumped the lot.'

He did not feel it necessary to explain that he had tipped all the chemicals into old Clem's well.